"Thanks for looking out for me."

"Anytime, Lex. Anytime."

Their fingers tangled together as she aligned her hand with his. But just as quickly as the simple touch of her hand began to feel like something more, she pulled away and hurried toward the garage where the lab vans were kept.

Aiden could still feel the warmth of her skin against his as he watched her walk away. A familiar pull in his gut followed right along with her. She waved over her shoulder before disappearing through the door and breaking the heated connection he fought to ignore.

Wanting the one woman he'd promised to be a brother to—and doing nothing about it—might well be the toughest challenge he'd ever tackled. And he'd been a cop for twelve years.

Still, Aiden would get the job done.

Even if that meant protecting Lexi from him.

He patted the dog beside him. "Come on, Blue. Let's go to work."

D0950147

K-9 PATROL

USA TODAY Bestselling Author
JULIE MILLER

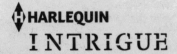

HARLEQUIN

INTRIGUE

For all the first responders and caregivers who gave so much to help
us get through 2020. Thank you.

With special thanks for my readers who helped me with my research:
Jennifer Lorenz Mewes, Mary Birchwood Lawson and Danelle Koch!

And a special thank-you to the real director of the KCPD Crime Lab,
Kevin Winer, who answered all my questions and sparked some ideas.
I appreciate that he allowed me to take some liberties with
my fictional story. Any mistakes are mine.

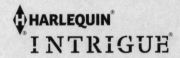

ISBN-13: 978-1-335-55542-7

K-9 Patrol

Recycling programs
for this product may
not exist in your area.

Harlequin Enterprises ULC
22 Adelaide St. West, 40th Floor
Toronto, Ontario M5H 4E3, Canada
www.Harlequin.com

Printed in U.S.A.

Julie Miller is an award-winning *USA TODAY* bestselling author of breathtaking romantic suspense—with a National Readers' Choice Award and a Daphne du Maurier Award, among other prizes. She has also earned an *RT Book Reviews* Career Achievement Award. For a complete list of her books, monthly newsletter and more, go to juliemiller.org.

Books by Julie Miller

Harlequin Intrigue

Kansas City Crime Lab

K-9 Patrol

The Taylor Clan: Firehouse 13

Crime Scene Cover-Up
Dead Man District

The Precinct

Beauty and the Badge
Takedown
KCPD Protector
Crossfire Christmas
Military Grade Mistletoe
Kansas City Cop

Rescued by the Marine
Do-or-Die Bridesmaid
Personal Protection
Target on Her Back
K-9 Protector
A Stranger on Her Doorstep

Visit the Author Profile page at Harlequin.com.

CAST OF CHARACTERS

Officer Aiden Murphy—Barely surviving his childhood, Aiden was taken in by the Callahan family. His debt of honor to them means watching over Lexi while her brother is deployed. Luckily he and his K-9 partner work in the same KCPD complex where Lexi works. But he can't ignore feelings that are anything but brotherly.

Lexi Callahan—Newly promoted, Lexi is supervisor of her own squad at the Kansas City Crime Lab. She needs to mold her unit into a cohesive team, string together the clues from a series of murders and stay alive when the killer targets her. But all that might be easier than guarding her heart against Aiden.

Blue—Aiden's K-9 partner, a black and tan Belgian Malinois. Besides Aiden, Lexi is his favorite human.

Levi Callahan—Lexi's big brother is a Marine deployed to the Middle East.

Mac Taylor—Lexi's boss at the crime lab.

Ethan Wynn—The voice of experience on Lexi's forensic team.

Shane Duvall—The nerdy professor on the forensic team.

Dennis Hunt—Lexi replaced him at the crime lab.

Kevin Nelson—Lexi's ex-boyfriend.

Jennifer Li—Who benefits from her death? And how far will the killer go to hide his involvement with her?

Chapter One

"Me?"

Criminalist Lexi Callahan pressed her lips together, just to make sure her mouth wasn't gaping open as she looked across the hallway to her boss, Mac Taylor, who ran the Kansas City Police Department Crime Laboratory. When he'd stopped her on the way to the break room near the end of her shift, she'd assumed he was asking for a favor or following up on her most recent crime scene analysis report—not that he was going to offer her a promotion.

Mac adjusted his glasses over his scarred face and smiled. "Don't sound so surprised. You've earned the job. I think Supervisor Lexi Callahan has a nice ring to it. True, you'll be stuck on the night shift sometimes, but you'd be running your own squad in the CSIU, reporting directly to Captain Stockman, sitting in on a meeting with me every now and then so I know what's going on at the front lines."

The boss of her own team. Coordinating the

jobs of gathering evidence and funneling it to the seven divisions and seventy or so experts who worked on everything from digital evidence to weapons identification, from bloodstain spatter analysis to microchemistry, DNA and more.

Lexi leaned back against the steel railing that ran the length of the windows lining the long hallway and common areas that connected the individual labs and crime lab offices on the west side of the building complex to the Seventh Precinct offices of KCPD on the east. She needed to sit, and she wasn't going to make it to a chair in the memorial lounge, where she and her colleagues often met to decompress from the stresses of the day. "Dennis is okay with this?" Her current B squad supervisor might be a stellar investigator, but he had been reprimanded, fined and ordered to attend sensitivity training to break his habit of calling the women on his team *honey* and *sweetie*, and finding subtle ways to *accidentally* make unnecessary contact with them.

"Dennis doesn't get a say in this. His tenure has left morale fractured around here. He's a liability to this entire department. I can fire him if he doesn't complete the training or picks up his old habits again. Right now, I just need to get him off the front line. There are trust issues that need to be mended around here. I think you're the woman for the job."

No pressure there. Lexi inhaled a steadying breath and nodded.

"Dennis is moving over into an administrative position, opening up the squad supervisor spot sooner than we were expecting." Kick Dennis off investigative work and stick him in an office where he had less chance of offending anyone until he hit retirement in a couple of years? Probably a wise decision for both staff morale and public relations. Putting a woman in charge would no doubt also alleviate some of the concerns from the women on staff. "These days, we're all more specialized than criminalists were when I first started. But you have training in multiple specialties, so I believe that gives you a unique understanding into the challenges each member of the lab faces. There's no one I trust more to bring in what we need from a crime scene. And if you can't get these guys thinking like a team again, I don't know who can."

Lexi tucked a chin-length wave of golden-brown hair behind her ear. "I'm flattered, sir."

"Don't be flattered. Be good." His phone must have vibrated in his pocket, because he held up a finger to pause the conversation a moment while he took it out and read a text.

While Mac answered the summons, Lexi looked to her coworkers in the lounge. Chemists and toxicologists. A nearsighted nerd with crazy mad computer skills. A blood expert who'd lost his legs in a war zone and now sat in a wheel-chair. He was playing chess with a man whose prematurely graying hair made him seem older than she knew him to be. There was an ogre-sized sharps expert standing off to himself who'd said maybe ten words to her outside of a case and had yet to meet a weapon he didn't recognize. The uniformed Black police sergeant who assisted Mac Taylor with administrative duties was chatting with a man who, like him, appeared to be in his midforties. The stranger looked like he could be a cop himself, although he wore a suit and tie beneath his winter coat. She'd seen him on the crime lab campus before, although she'd never met him.

She counted many of them among her friends. Other than the man who looked like a bulldog and was chatting with Sergeant King, they were all her coworkers. "I'd be in charge of them? That's a lot of different personalities to deal with. A couple of them have been here longer than I have. Won't they resent me getting the promotion ahead of them?"

"Some of them don't want the job. They're happier in the lab than out in the field. And not a one of them has your people skills." Mac pocketed his phone and continued the sales pitch. "I'm not going to lie to you—people will need time to adjust to your changing role in their world. And how you deal with certain situations could impact those relationships. But if everyone is mature about it and remembers we're a team and we're here to help KCPD solve crimes, you can still be friends. But now you're also their boss. After the issues with Dennis, my hope is that smart, trustworthy leadership will help this unit gel into a stronger team."

"You believe I can do that?"

Mac's good eye narrowed as he debated whether or not that had been a rhetorical question. "Yes."

Stuff like this didn't happen to her. Nothing much ever happened to Alexis Sedell Callahan. Not since her parents had been murdered during a carjacking her junior year of high school. Her overprotective big brother, who'd stepped up to parent her, had seen to that. Levi Callahan was a six-foot-two Marine with green eyes that matched her own. Lexi adored her brother, who, whether he was stateside or deployed across the world, seemed to find a way to keep his eye on her.

That protective streak had only increased after her college sweetheart had cheated on her shortly after moving in with her. He claimed she'd become a workaholic, with no time for his needs. She'd been holding down a full-time job and attending grad school at the time. Kevin Nelson had wanted them to work in his father's pharmaceutical company together, but she'd opted for public service at the crime lab. She'd been inspired by Mac Taylor himself, after his work at the lab had identified the meth head who had shot her parents. His scientific investigation had helped get the killer sent to prison so he couldn't hurt any more families the way he'd destroyed hers.

Now *she* was the one helping the police, uncovering and analyzing clues, solidifying cases so KCPD could make arrests and the DA could prosecute the perps and make Kansas City safer. If it were in her power, no one else would suffer the kind of loss she and her brother, Levi, had and not find justice.

The crime lab was where she needed to be, where she wanted to be.

If she could make it even better by taking charge of a small part of it, then she'd do that, too.

She waited until Mac had finished the texting that was making him smile before continuing the conversation. "I thought you were calling me in to ask me to cover someone's shift over the Thanksgiving holiday this week. I know you always have a big, multigenerational family deal, and I'm...alone...this year, so I'm available. I didn't realize the board had finished interviewing the candidates and made their decision so quickly."

"Dennis's actions sped the process."

No doubt. She'd been one of the women who'd

filed a grievance against her supervisor. "The science and administrative duties I can handle. It's the team management I have to consider. I thought the interview was more of a learning exercise, building experience for me."

"Then you shouldn't have killed it."

"Well, I didn't mean to do such a good job." Maybe she shouldn't be making sarcastic jokes with the boss. "I mean, thank you, sir."

He chuckled and slipped his fingers through his graying blond hair. "Your brother's still deployed?"

Lexi nodded. "He's based in Afghanistan right now. He gets leave over Christmas. We're going to celebrate all the holidays then. As the newest squad leader, will I be on call over Christmas?"

Mac seemed to understand that she had several things to consider before giving him a firm answer. "You've got a couple of days to think it over. I'll make sure you get time off at Christmas while your brother is home. But I'd like your first shift as squad supervisor to start on the twenty-seventh."

"Thanksgiving Day," she confirmed.

"That gives you two days to decide."

Lexi pushed herself off the railing. "Thank you for the opportunity, sir. I'll let you know ASAP."

Mac nodded. Then he held up his phone and smiled. Although he was blind in one eye, following an explosion in the city's first crime lab, his good eye sparkled as he mentioned his family. "My wife has informed me that our daughter's basketball tournament is about to tip off, and I am not there. I'd better obey the boss and get over to the high school."

Lexi chuckled. She'd had the pleasure of meeting Mac's wife, Julia, at a few work functions, and her impression of the experienced trauma nurse was that she was a gentle, kind soul who was anything but bossy. And it was clear Mac adored her. Lexi ignored the pang of longing that tried to take hold inside her. After she'd dumped Kevin, and her brother had stepped up to screen out anyone he didn't deem good enough for his little sister, it looked like her hope for finding a similar forever relationship of her own would be taking a back seat to her career indefinitely. Good thing she loved what she was doing and didn't need a man to make her happy. Although, that lonely space around her heart wasn't above wanting someone special in her life in addition to a successful, meaningful career.

Suspecting this conversation had already gone on longer than Mac had intended, Lexi sent him on his way. He didn't need to stand here and wait while she deliberated the pros and cons of accepting this promotion right now. "You'd better get out of here, then. Tell Jules hi."

"Will do." He inclined his head toward the break room. "You'd better check in with your entourage. I think they're curious about what we're discussing out here."

Lexi turned to see several of her coworkers' conversations had stopped and they were looking toward the hallway where she and Mac stood. Although most of them quickly glanced away and feigned a sudden interest in coffee mugs, snacks and whoever was standing or sitting closest to them, she hadn't missed their inquisitive looks. With an embarrassed sigh and a shake of her head, she glanced up at Mac. "Sorry about that."

"Don't be. The only place news travels faster than around the Seventh Precinct/Crime Lab is between my mom and mother-in-law." He arched a golden brow above the rim of his glasses. "Good luck if you're heading in there."

"They probably want to know if anyone else is getting transferred or fired. I'll stop the rumor mill before it starts. Good night, sir."

"Good night, Lexi." He pointed a finger at her, even as he was backing toward his office to grab his winter coat and lock up. "Two days and I'll need that decision."

Two days to change the status quo of her utterly predictable life and take on the burden of safe, trustworthy leadership for all those worried souls in the break room and beyond. Right. No pressure at all.

Lexi exhaled a deep breath before she strolled to the lounge. Jackson Dobbs, who looked more like a defensive lineman for the Kansas City Chiefs than the sharps and ballistics expert he was, filled the doorway. He stepped back as though he'd been ready to leave but hadn't wanted to pass by and interrupt her conversation with their boss. Lexi moved past him to find her coworkers all staring at her again. "You guys saw me talking to Mac? It's not what you think. No one's getting fired."

"Well, duh." Chelsea O'Brien pushed her glasses up onto the bridge of her freckled nose. "Okay, yes, that's what we were thinking at first. At least, I was. But then, Jackson was standing right by the door, so he heard the actual words and was eavesdropping for us." She paused for a breath. "Now we know. You're taking the job, right?"

Jackson Dobbs, the man who gave *stoic* its definition in the dictionary, had been relaying gossip? She tilted her gaze up to the icy gray eyes of the man who towered above her. "*You* were spying on me?"

He shrugged.

Chelsea got up from the tall table where she'd been working on her laptop and pointed to the hallway just outside the lounge. "You were right there. And, you know, Jackson doesn't miss much."

Khari Thomas's long ebony braids stirred across her shoulders as she adjusted her white lab coat over her pregnant belly. "We made him do it." She crossed the lounge to elbow Jackson's arm and take the sting out of her words. "Although, he was annoyingly short on details. One word. One stinkin' word. *Promotion.* We filled in the rest. Congratulations, Lexi. I'm going to like working for a woman for a change. Especially after Dennis." She cupped her extended belly with both hands. "You'd think with him having a new fiancée, and me carrying this basketball, he'd stop looking at my butt."

Lexi swept her gaze around the room. "You guys all know?"

Grayson Malone spun his wheelchair away from the chess game to face her. "We're some of the smartest people on the planet." The veteran Marine scratched at the dark blond stubble blanketing his angular jawline. "We know Hunt is on his way out. It's not that tricky a mystery to solve. Take the job."

Ethan Wynn was a handsome man despite his prematurely graying hair. Since the two of them had gone through orientation at the same time and worked the CSIU together ever since, she didn't mind when he pulled her in for a quick hug. "Congrats, Lexi. Well deserved."

She smiled up into his brown eyes as she pulled away. "Thanks, Ethan. I know you interviewed for the promotion, too. I'm sure you'll be offered the next spot that opens up."

He shrugged off the compliment. "It's a sensitive time for the lab. I can see why a woman is the smart choice for the job right now. Besides, *you'll* get to deal with the transition hiccups and spike in crimes over the holidays, not me." He winked and grinned before turning back to the table and moving his bishop across the chessboard. "I'm holding out for Taylor's position, anyway. The guy's gotta retire one of these days, doesn't he?"

Not anytime soon, she hoped. She couldn't imagine a better mentor teaching her the ropes if she did agree to the supervisory position.

Lexi opened the insulated mug she'd carried into the break room and went to refill it for the drive home. But the pot was empty. Not one to leave a job unfinished, she opened the machine to dump the used grounds and refill it with fresh beans from the cabinet above her. Not only would the next shift be looking for coffee when they reported for work in about twenty minutes, but she needed the jolt to the brain to help organize all the thoughts running through her head. Once the pot started to fill with the fresh, fragrant brew, she turned to face her friends again. "You all think you can take orders from me?"

Gray moved his king to a safe position on the board. "Are you going to be more like my mother or my drill sergeant?"

Chelsea ran over and linked their elbows, standing shoulder to shoulder with her. "She's going to be like Lexi. The team's going to stick together and it's all going to be fine." Today,

Chelsea's hazel eyes were circled by tiny turkeys dancing around the frames of her orange glasses. "Seriously, I thought Mac might be transferring you to a different shift. Breaking up the team."

"I haven't taken the job yet."

Shane Duvall, whose narrow black glasses were more "nerdy professor" than Chelsea's seasonal eyewear, fit the stereotype of a scientist and lab technician better than any of them. Supremely logical, he'd probably already created a pros and cons list inside his head. "Why not? I don't see any downside to you running the show. I appreciated your help with the chemical analysis on the Norwell case. And your suggestion that I submit the formula to the state fire office to add to their database, as well, was spot-on. That sort of interdepartmental teamwork will only continue with you at the helm."

"You guys." She looked from face to face, overwhelmed by their show of support. Of course, this was the grace period. The first time she had to reprimand one of them or stick them with an assignment he or she didn't like, they might rethink their friendship with her. "We have different strengths, work in different departments. And we've been on the same level for a long time. It's going to change the dynamic between us."

Jackson finally spoke from his position at the door. "Why?"

"Jackson's right." Gray seemed to speak a code with the big guy, understanding far more than the words Jackson actually said. "With the exception of one divisive clunker who's tried to undermine several of us, the KCPD Crime Lab is a well-oiled machine. We do good work. Shifting our job assignments a little shouldn't alter that. You pretty much keep us organized and on task already. Now you're getting the pay grade to match."

Rufus King came up on the other side of Lexi and touched her shoulder to get her attention. Then he extended his hand to shake hers. "About time they recognized your talent, Ms. Callahan. Congratulations."

"I haven't said yes yet."

"Robert Buckner." Rufus's friend extended his hand, as well. "Why not? You seem to be the only one hesitating here. Congratulations, by the way."

"Um, thank you?"

Rufus explained the stocky man's presence in the lounge. "Buck was my partner before I transferred to the lab to help run the admin side of things. He left the force about the same time. Now he's got his own private investigation firm—still does some odd jobs for the department."

Odd jobs? What did that mean?

"In return, we help him out when we can."

Help? In what way? But before she could ask specifically what had brought Buck to the crime lab, or what his definition of an *odd job* entailed, Rufus nudged his former partner toward the exit. "Come on, Buck. Let's let these young pups stew over the decisions that you and I already know the answers to. Besides, you owe me a dinner. I'm thinking steak, since my wife will be feeding me every incarnation of turkey for the next two weeks."

"Mr. Buckner?" Chelsea stopped the man with the salt-and-pepper hair before he headed out with Rufus. "I've got that file you gave me downloaded onto my computer. I'll work on tracking down the information you asked for in my spare time. Around my duties here at the lab, of course. We won't let it be a cold case forever. I promise."

What kind of quid pro quo was going on here? And what did it have to do with the lab's top computer expert using her skills to help a civilian, even if he was a former cop?

Robert Buckner patted Chelsea's hand where it rested on the sleeve of his wool coat. "Thank you, Miss O'Brien. Any help you can give me, I'd appreciate."

"Sure thing. And it's Chelsea. Or Chels. I answer to both. Any friend of Sergeant King's is a friend of mine. And, you know, I do have spare time. Too much of it, really. That's why I'm online so much instead of hanging out with real people. Except for the folks here. I mean, they're real people, obviously… Um, okay. TMI."

To his credit, the older man focused on everything she was saying until her nerves kicked in and she pulled away to needlessly adjust her glasses again. "Thank you… Chelsea," he responded in a gruff voice. "I'll be in touch."

Chelsea's lips buzzed with a long exhalation as the two older men left the lounge. "That was awkward. Of course it was awkward. *I* was talking. I was rambling."

"Easy, Chels," Lexi teased, knowing enough about Chelsea's people-pleasing personality to suspect it hadn't taken much persuasion to secure her cooperation. Although Lexi was sensitive to her coworker's insecurities, she was also protective of the friend who seemed to be even more alone in the world than she was. Was Robert Buckner taking advantage of the resident computer geek's big heart? "What's with you and the private detective?"

Chelsea's hazel eyes darted to Lexi's. "Oh. I can't say. I promised to be discreet. It's an old case that he needs solved. He's not much for computers, but he thinks I might be able to dig up a connection somebody missed." Her gaze swung back to the men disappearing down the hallway. "He's lost a lot, and he seems so sad with those big puppy dog eyes." Um, *puppy dog* was not the descriptor Lexi had thought of when she'd looked at the stocky man hanging out with Rufus. "I need him to smile. When Sergeant King asked me if I could help his ex-partner do some research, I wanted to."

While Lexi felt this personal request required a little more digging into to make sure that neither the lab nor Chelsea herself was being compromised, the frown line above the brunette's glasses made her think her friend was the sad one here. Lexi dropped a comforting arm around Chelsea's shoulders. "Hey, if it's anything to do with cyberspace, then he's come to the right person."

Chelsea grinned at the praise. "See? That's exactly the kind of thing a good supervisor would say to her team. That makes me feel like I can really help him. You're a natural."

"Yeah, well, whatever you're doing for him— it's not impacting your work for the lab, is it?"

Lexi never got an answer for that one. Chelsea clapped her hands together and gasped with delight. "Speaking of puppy dog eyes… Blue!"

A muscular brown dog with a black face and dark eyes strutted into the lounge. He rubbed past Jackson Dobbs's legs, pushed his nose into Khari Thomas's hand and accepted a pat on the flank from Shane Duvall, before stopping at Grayson Malone's wheelchair for a scratch around his pricked ears. If it wasn't for the brass badge clipped to his collar, a stranger might mistake the

Belgian Malinois police officer for some kind of therapy dog because he stopped to greet and be adored by everyone in the room. That was, until Chelsea called his name and his sharp-eyed attention shifted to her. The working dog's tongue lolled out of his mouth as he panted with anticipation and hurried over to them.

Lexi scrubbed her palms against the dog's jowls, smiling at the way he huffed with the excitement he felt at the familiar caress. Petting and playing with the high-energy dog added joy to Lexi's afternoon, too.

But it was Blue's partner, Aiden Murphy, exchanging greetings just outside the lounge, who captured Lexi's attention.

"Murph."

"Sarge. Buck."

Lexi looked straight across the room to meet deep blue eyes focused squarely on her.

One of those blue eyes winked. "Congratulations on your promotion."

The deep-pitched drawl that was colored with a hint of Aiden's Irish ancestors when he hit his *r*'s danced against her eardrums. Although she managed to keep her tongue in her mouth, Lexi's pulse fluttered with a silent echo of the excitement Blue was displaying as he rolled over onto his back to give Chelsea access to his chest and belly. The uniformed officer in the doorway was the real reason she had almost no social life, and why her ex-boyfriend and any other man who might be remotely interested in her barely got the chance to date her, much less get involved enough to hurt her.

Aiden Murphy, KCPD K-9 officer. Six feet of lean muscle put together with the same sinewy athleticism as the well-trained dog who lived and worked with him every day. Blue-black hair cropped close enough on the sides that you could see his scalp. He had a tiny scar on his chin and imperfect features that his easy smile and killer blue eyes transformed into a compellingly masculine face. Her brother's best friend. Substitute big brother whenever Levi was overseas.

The man who would never know how seriously close she'd come to letting him break her heart growing up.

Chapter Two

Aiden didn't question the tension easing from his chest when he saw Lexi's smile and the way she wrestled playfully with his dog. Silky, toffee-colored waves danced around her chin as she shook her head at his dramatic wink. Maybe he'd overreacted by jogging through the gym and common areas connecting the precinct offices with the crime lab to see for himself that she was all right. But he was who he was. He was a protective man by nature and training—and he was majorly protective of all things Callahan.

News traveled fast through the crime lab and precinct offices. Any gossip that included Lexi Callahan's name merited an investigation.

The trouble with gossip was that the story changed from telling to telling. He'd prepared to do battle against the reprimand he'd first erroneously heard about, but his outrage was quickly replaced with a sense of pride when he'd learned that she wasn't in trouble at all. She'd been tapped to head up her own squad at the lab. But his concern had reawakened when someone reported that she was hesitating to take the promotion. Why? Lexi was smart, funny, caring and independent; she made the people in her circle more confident and capable just by being around them. *He* was a better man for knowing her.

They were so talking about this. He'd spent eight years of his life with the Callahans. Eight years in which he had three meals a day, a warm bed, and he didn't have to sleep with his too tight shoes and threadbare coat on in case the night went to hell and he had to run away to a place where the adults weren't yelling or using him as a punching bag. Even though they shared no blood ties, Leroy and Lila Callahan, Levi and Lexi were more family to him than his own father and stepmothers had ever been. And now that Mr. and Mrs. Callahan had tragically been taken from them, and Lexi was on her own stateside, he'd promised her brother, Levi, that she would make smart decisions and lead a safe, successful life while he was away serving his country in the Middle East.

Lexi was family. Sort of like a sister. Certainly a friend.

And it was killing him.

Her irritation with his cheesy wink gave way to a teasing laugh as she watched Blue work the room. "I see you brought your better-looking half."

"Ha ha." Aiden strolled into the employee lounge, exchanging a nod with Jackson and Khari. He shook hands with Gray and Ethan, and doffed a salute to Shane, following the same path his partner had taken toward Lexi.

By the time he reached them, Blue was on his back and Chelsea O'Brien was on her knees exchanging sloppy face licks for fingernails scratching his chest and belly. "Hey, Aiden." Chelsea glanced up briefly before a slurp against her jaw swung her attention back to the dog. "It's okay if I pet Blue, isn't it?"

"You bet." Aiden leaned his hip against the counter beside Lexi, wondering who was enjoying themselves more—his partner or the computer genius. "He's off duty right now, and you're on the short list of people he likes. I think Blue's got a thing for the ladies." The Belgian Malinois might be all adrenaline and intensity on the job, but he was a sucker for soft hands and a pretty face. He couldn't blame the pooch, really. What full-blooded male wouldn't want Lexi Callahan putting her hands on him? Lexi wasn't the one with her hands on the dog now, and still his thoughts had gone there. Aiden gripped the counter behind him and looked out the bank of windows into the grayish light of the muted sunset until he could shut down that unbidden thought and remember why he'd come here in the first place. He blinked once, then looked over his shoulder at Lexi. "Why won't you take the job?"

She sank back against the counter beside him. "Not you, too."

"Of course me, too." He matched her stance, crossing his arms over his protective utility vest, where he wore his badge, radio, spare ammo magazines, Taser and other gear. He wore his gun strapped to his thigh. "I feel like I'm part of this lab. Blue and I are the primary protection team assigned to watch your backs out in the field. Maybe you guys don't wear a badge and gun like me, but that doesn't make me any less a part of this team. Take the job."

Lexi leaned a little closer, until her arm brushed against his and she could tilt her cheek against his shoulder and drop her voice to a whisper. "I wouldn't be stepping into an easy situation."

Aiden ignored the scents of milk and honey and some sort of laboratory disinfectant coming off her hair and clothes, and dipped his head to match her whisper. "These are good people. Give 'em a chance."

"I'm not worried about *them*."

He frowned as she straightened away from him. He'd never liked when the overachiever he'd grown up with sold herself short. "You take on more than a normal person should. You over-think your decision until you lose sleep and give yourself a headache. Then you kick butt and do a great job anyway." Aiden shrugged. He wasn't the brains of this relationship, but the logic seemed simple to him. "Just skip to the kick-butt part."

Lexi pushed away from the counter to step in front of him and face him, still whispering. "You think I can do this."

"I know you can."

"Back to work, everybody." Another uniformed officer rapped on the door frame, diverting everyone's attention to his arrival. Captain Brian Stockman was one of the two sworn officers on the crime lab staff. While Rufus King liaised the administrative offices of the lab with KCPD, Captain Stockman ran the CSIU, coordinating the work the criminalists did out in the field with the officers and detectives investigating the cases. Only Mac Taylor was more senior on staff, so if Captain Stockman said to move out, they all fell into line. "Unfortunately, you all are still on the clock until the next shift comes on. We need a field team to roll. We've got a break-in with a DB in one of the hotels downtown."

While Stockman's rank earned him respect, his close-shaved graying hair only added to his air of authority, as far as Aiden was concerned. But the tall, lanky man with the obvious hair plugs compensating for his thinning gray-blond hair who pushed his way past Captain Stockman didn't seem to share that same respect.

Dennis Hunt waltzed into the break room. "I hate to break up this party I wasn't invited to." His dark eyes skirted past Aiden and zeroed in on Lexi. "Callahan. You're with me. Dobbs? You, too."

To Blue's chagrin, Chelsea scrambled to her feet, and grabbed her laptop and backpack. "Gotta go. See ya, Lexi. 'Bye, Aiden."

"Miss O'Brien." Dennis's greeting, laced with a subtle amusement, made Chelsea duck her head and scuttle past him out the door.

Aiden grabbed the dog's collar and ordered Blue into a sit when he would have followed the other woman into the hallway. "Is she okay?"

"She'll be fine," Lexi assured him, but he wasn't sure he believed her. "She's one of us who filed a harassment grievance against him. I hooked her up with the staff counselor to talk about it. Dennis seems to bring out the fight-or-flight instinct in all of us."

Aiden's reaction was the curling-his-fingers-into-a-fist variety. There were a lot of things about Chelsea that reminded him of his early childhood, where trust and security had been an option. But where he'd grown tough, gotten physical and trained to take on the world, her insecurities seemed to have made her skittish and fearful. This guy must have one hell of a lawyer and a ton of tenure to still be employed after the stories he'd heard. Of course, Hunt had never been promoted beyond field supervisor, and never would be, so the man was paying for his unacceptable choices in other ways.

When Hunt crossed the room to pour himself a cup of freshly brewed coffee, Blue followed Aiden's nonverbal cue and positioned himself between Lexi and her soon-to-be ex-boss. Hair-plug man ignored the defensive perimeter and spoke to Lexi. "I know Taylor offered you my position. Bet you've already got plans for redecorating my office. But for two more days, I'm still running this squad and giving out the assignments. So come on, sweetie. Let's move it. You and Jumbo are pulling the long shift with me."

Aiden's instinct to shut Hunt up was cut short by the hand that snaked around his forearm. Lexi's touch silently warned him that she could handle this without his help. As quickly as she had touched him, she pulled away to settle her hand on top of Blue's head. Did she worry the dog was as primed to attack as Aiden was? Or was she letting the dog center her? Cool her temper or buck up her strength?

"Sweetie?" He recognized the snap in that tone. "I take it you haven't started your sensitivity training class. Or do I need to file another complaint against you?"

"Just keep 'em coming, honey. You haven't got rid of me yet."

She crossed her arms in front of her. "Is that a challenge?"

Jackson Dobbs suddenly filled up the space on the other side of her. Although he didn't protest like she did, Aiden assumed the big guy didn't appreciate the nickname, either.

Hunt was smart enough, at least, not to take on all four of them. He put his hand up in an insincere apology. "Sorry. Pseudo-Supervisor Callahan, would you move your...?" He thought better of that choice of word. "Would you please hurry? I have plans with Bertie tonight, and I want to get this dead hooker scene processed ASAP."

Lexi didn't say another word until Hunt had left the room. "Wow. You don't think he's bitter, do you? He destroys his own career and thinks he can blame me?" Her tone was almost as snarky as Hunt's had been. "This is going to be a fun evening."

Jackson gave Lexi's arm a sympathetic squeeze before heading out. "I'll get the van warmed up. Meet you out back. Take the job."

Had Aiden ever heard the weapons expert string so many words together in a single conversation? But while Lexi seemed equally surprised by the big man's vote of confidence, Aiden had a more immediate issue to discuss. Now that the room had cleared except for Lexi, Aiden and his K-9 partner, Aiden blocked Lexi's path to the exit and faced her. "Please say I can punch Hunt in the mouth for the way he talks to you."

"And make me write you up on the report, too? That's the kind of attitude I'm supposed to fix." She stepped around him and headed down the hallway. "Besides, if anybody's punching him, I'm doing it."

"That's my girl." Aiden grinned and tapped his thigh, and Blue fell into step beside him as he followed Lexi into her tiny office. He and Blue waited in the doorway while she pulled her coat and crime scene kit from the closet behind her desk. "Now explain to me why you didn't jump on Mac's offer to take over Hunt's job." She set the kit on her desk and eyed him with a silent question. "News travels fast around this place. Anyone would be an improvement over that guy."

"Gee, thanks."

"You know what I mean. B squad would be lucky to have you running the team." He gestured with his thumb over his shoulder to the hallway where the others had gone back to their labs and offices. "If Big Jack mentioned it, then you know they think so, too."

Lexi shrugged into her insulated coat. "They're being nice because they're my friends."

"They're being nice because they know you've earned the promotion and they believe you can make them feel like they're safe in their own workspace. They respect you in ways they'll never be able to respect Hunt again."

"You're sure this isn't just your big brother instincts kicking in?" He stiffened at the brotherly appellation. "I know you promised Levi you'd keep an eye on me while he's deployed. You pulled my car out of the ditch when I hit that patch of ice. Fixed the leaky faucet in my kitchen. Apparently, that mandate means advising me on career moves, too."

"Lex—"

"I'm a grown-up, Aiden. Hell, I'm thirty years old. I can weigh the pros and cons myself without you or Levi telling me what to do. Supervising Criminalist means better pay. More seniority. More responsibility. I'm sure Levi would see it as a step in the right direction for my career. It means job security in his eyes. *Life* security." She pulled on a black knit stocking cap with the letters *CSI* embroidered on the front. "I'd be on the right track to everything Levi wants for me."

"What do *you* want?"

"I want the job. I want to keep making a difference. I want to erase the memory of everything Dennis has said and done and put my own stamp on this lab. But what if I'm not ready for that? What if I screw it up and make things worse? I already lead a pretty solitary existence." She worked her bottom lip between her teeth and glanced beyond him to the hallway where the others had passed by. "What if I lose the friends I do have in the process?"

"You'll always have me." Her eyes widened at that instinctive reply, and the room was silent for several uncomfortably long seconds. Wow. Did that sound as lovelorn-loser pathetic to Lexi's ears as it did to his own? *Turn it into a joke, Murph. Make her smile.* "And Blue." He reached down to scrub his hand over Blue's head. "As long as you're handing out tummy rubs, you'll never get rid of Blue."

Lexi visibly relaxed. Her teeth released the lip she'd worried, and she gave him that familiar smile as she crossed the room to pet Blue, too. "That's the kind of loyalty I want the staff to have with me. You should have heard them. They think changing supervisors is going to make everything right again. But it's not going to happen in a day. They might not be working one-on-one with Dennis anymore, but he'll still be around unless he does something else stupid to get himself fired. I'd have to run interference in the meantime. That's a lot of pressure."

Aiden inhaled a deep breath, steeling himself to play the part he'd promised. "I don't have to be a stand-in big brother for my best friend to know this is a great opportunity for you. You'll figure out your management style as you go along. Even Mac still goes out in the field sometimes, so clearly, you're not going to be stuck behind a desk. You'll still get to do the job you love. Work side by side with the people who mean something to you."

Lexi straightened to zip her coat. "I'll just have more job to do. More assignments to organize and prioritize. More people to wrangle. More favors to call in and problems to listen to and egos to soothe."

"Nobody can handle the responsibility better than you. I grew up with you and Levi. I know you." The ends of her hair curled beneath the edge of the stocking cap, and he gave in to the urge to capture a strand that clung to the corner of her mouth and brush it back into place along her jaw. "Your brother may be the Marine, but I know who the real tough guy is in the Callahan family. You're taking the job, Lex. I can already see it in your eyes."

She planted her hands on her hips and tilted her face to his. "Okay, Mr. Know-It-All. What are my eyes saying now?"

He'd memorized every shade of moss, juniper and jade in her pretty green eyes. Knew what almost every nuance of color and expression meant, and he was reading this one loud and clear. He was pushing her too hard when she needed time to process her thoughts.

"That I'm not getting invited over for Thanksgiving dinner?" Even though she snickered at the joke, he wisely retreated into the hallway. "Fine.

I get the message. Back off. I'll get Blue geared up and meet you at the crime scene to clear it before you go to work."

She picked up her kit, switched off the light and locked the door behind her.

Aiden turned and walked backward until she caught up to him. "And, hey, stick with Dobbs until I get there. I don't want you spending any time alone with Hunt if you can help it."

"Neither do I." She caught his hand and squeezed his fingers to stop him from turning toward the precinct side of the complex. "And, Aiden? I know Levi calls and checks in with you from time to time. Don't say anything to him about the new job, okay? I want to tell him."

"Roger that."

"Thanks for looking out for me."

"Anytime, Lex. Anytime."

Their fingers tangled together as she aligned her hand with his. But just as quickly as the simple touch of her hand began to feel like something more, she pulled away and hurried toward the garage, where the lab vans were kept.

Aiden could still feel the warmth of her skin against his as he watched her walk away. A familiar pull in his gut followed right along with her. She waved over her shoulder before disappearing through the door and breaking the heated connection he fought to ignore.

Nothing like lusting after forbidden fruit. Levi

had entrusted her care to him. *Protect my sister. Make sure she's safe and happy. Don't let any man hurt her.* Not Dennis Hunt. Not a criminal. Not a lover. Aiden had given his word. They'd shaken hands on it.

Aiden was alive today because of the Callahan family. Because of Lexi's parents and her big brother, he wasn't in jail, he wasn't dead, and he hadn't become an alcoholic loser like his abusive father, who hadn't even known that when Aiden wasn't in school he had been living on the streets before Levi found him and took him home. The Callahans had saved him in every way that mattered. He owed them.

If Levi wanted him to look out for Lexi the same way he would if he were stateside, then Aiden would do it.

But that promise was exacting a price from him. He hadn't been able to make a serious relationship with any woman work for a few years now. And he'd dated some nice ones. But it hadn't seemed fair to pretend he could do forever when a piece of his heart belonged to Lexi. Maybe if he'd stuck with Patrick Murphy's neglect and drunken rages—maybe if he'd made it on the streets—he wouldn't feel the guilt warring with the desire inside him. Maybe that was all this was—desire. And if that was the case, then he'd keep his hands off Lexi. But if these were real feelings… Hell. He'd keep his heart to himself, too, because he'd made the damn promise. He'd be whatever Lexi and Levi needed him to be.

Wanting the one woman he'd vowed to be a brother to—and doing nothing about it—might well be the toughest assignment he'd ever tackled. And he'd been a cop for twelve years and had survived Patrick Murphy.

Still, Aiden would get the job done.

Even if that meant protecting Lexi from himself.

He patted the dog beside him. "Come on, Blue. Let's go to work."

Chapter Three

Thanksgiving

"Way to make a difference, Callahan," Lexi teased out loud, deciding to move the Advent calendar from the back of her office door, which she intended to leave open as much as possible, to the closet door, where she'd see it at least twice a day when she hung up or retrieved her coat. She was making some groundbreaking decisions on her first shift as supervisor in the nearly deserted lab complex. She reached into the box on her desk to unpack a colorful arrangement of frosted silk greenery and shiny red balls tucked into a mug painted like a snowman. "Now, where am I going to put this guy?"

The news feed from the mayor's Plaza lighting ceremony that took place every Thanksgiving night played on her phone on her desk, drowning out the echo of crickets chirping in the empty hallways. She'd taken a break from filling out paperwork and reading the policy and procedure manual to decorate her office for the holidays.

She'd wanted this job, right? She'd finally decided that she could be a better friend to Chelsea, Khari, Gray, Ethan and the others by being an advocate rather than just a buddy who shared coffee in the lounge with them and commiserated over inclusive test results, evidence that didn't make sense, or all the steps the department had to go through before giving Dennis Hunt his walking papers. She wanted to be good at her new position, to earn her team's respect. But she was off to an inauspicious start.

While there were four squads of criminalists covering the CSIU 24/7 or were available on call over the holidays, administrators and specialists who worked mostly in the lab itself had the day off. These were the people who ran analysis tests and database searches for ongoing investigations. Lexi had kept herself busy for a few hours, but the loneliness was starting to bounce off the walls and close in on her. Not that she'd have any company at home, either. No family, no pet, no boyfriend—just work and home alone. Seemed like her personal life was about as exciting as work this evening. She needed to meet someone, or join a group or activity where she could make friends outside of the lab. Maybe she should adopt a cat from one of the local shelters.

While she had Levi's arrival just before Christmas to look forward to, it was still a long stretch between Thanksgiving and Christmas. Then he'd be gone again right after the New Year, and she'd be all by herself again in that gorgeous rattletrap of a Craftsman home where she'd grown up.

Not that she'd had big plans for celebrating the holiday today, anyway. When she was younger, her parents had taken her and Levi, and then Aiden, too, down to the Plaza after a big Thanksgiving dinner every year. They'd wait with anticipation in the cold, with thousands of other Kansas Citians and tourists, for some local celebrity or lucky child to throw the switch and turn on over a million colorful lights strung along every storefront, roofline and dome in the historic J. C. Nichols Plaza shopping area south of downtown KC. After the decorations turned the shopping district into Christmas and the crowd cheered, they'd go for ice cream or hot chocolate, depending on the temperature. Then they'd walk around the shops to view their elaborate window displays. It wasn't just a Kansas City holiday tradition—it was a Callahan family tradition.

But then Levi had enlisted after graduation, Aiden had gone to a community college and the police academy, and she'd become a teenager too cool to hang with her parents. And then her parents were gone. After that was college, and more college, and work. She never seemed to find her way back to the Plaza to see the lighting ceremony in person, to feel the excitement in the air, to connect with the rest of the crowd and be inspired to celebrate the holiday season. For a while with her ex, Kevin, she'd thought she was getting back to personal connections and family and meaningful celebrations.

But soon she could see that Kevin didn't want the same things she did. Although they shared similar skill sets, she was a woman with a cause, and he wanted to go into the family pharmaceutical business and make money like his father. Even as they were drifting apart, she was fighting to make their relationship work. He wanted a business partner, or better yet, a trophy wife. She needed to feel more useful than that. She was a lab tech at heart. An investigator who liked piecing together clues and solving mysteries and making a difference—the way her parents had made a difference in the world, the way *she* made a difference here at the crime lab.

And finally, there was Kevin in bed with another woman in their new apartment, a slew of apologies, and a lame-ass marriage proposal complete with an impractical, gaudy diamond she wouldn't be able to wear to work, and promises she could no longer believe. The relationship had ended with the realization that she didn't know Kevin anymore, and maybe he'd never known the real Lexi at all.

So much for a family and a home and the holidays.

The snowman mug found a home on top of the file cabinet just as the countdown started on her phone. She sat on the corner of her desk to watch the live feed of the white, red, green and multicolored lights suddenly illuminating the Plaza landscape. She smiled at the festive beauty of it all, as well as the memories of Thanksgivings and Christmases past.

But just as the crowds started to disperse to visit a bar or restaurant, walk back to nearby hotel rooms or window-shop at the stores—there was no sense returning to their vehicles and driving home just yet, as the Plaza boulevards and side streets would be notoriously jammed with pedestrians and parked cars—the happy trip down memory lane faded and disappeared into the sterile white walls of her office. There might be thousands of people down on the Plaza, but she was alone in her office putting up a handful of Christmas decorations and waiting for something to happen.

Be careful what you wish for, Callahan.

The phone on her desk rang. After hours on a holiday meant only one thing. They'd caught a case. She quickly turned off the news feed on her cell and picked up the receiver. "Lexi Callahan. KCPD Crime Lab."

"Lexi—?" Captain Stockman covered the phone

and yelled at someone to turn down the game on the television before returning to the call. "First, happy Thanksgiving."

He seemed to need the greeting to cool his frustration and organize his thoughts. Lexi gave him that time. "Same to you, sir. I hope you and your family are enjoying the day."

"Ate too much. My team's losing. Doing great." She smiled a moment at the older man's deadpan delivery, but had her pen and notepad ready when he got down to business. "Who's there with you?"

"It's just me on site. But Ethan Wynn and Shane Duvall are on call."

"Good. Call them. We've got a murder down on the Plaza. The Regal Hotel." The prestigious historic brownstone was a name that she recognized. The Regal had played host to mobsters, politicians and celebrities throughout the years. Recently, it had been completely remodeled with every modern amenity, while keeping its historic charm. The pricey hotel had a gated entrance and parking lot, and boasted one of the best views of the city, with its floor-to-ceiling windows on the north side facing Brush Creek and the Plaza district down below. Those rooms didn't come cheaply over the holidays, and they were booked years in advance to ensure a warm, elegant place to hang out while enjoying an unobstructed view of the festivities down below.

Not the sort of place where she'd expect to process such a violent crime. "You're sure it's murder?"

"Well, the maid who discovered the body was pretty hysterical, so we didn't get much from her. But the first officers on the scene described indications of a fight and a ligature around the victim's neck."

"That's the same MO of the scene I processed on Monday." Although, the prostitute with fresh tracks in her arm and the by-the-hour room rental hardly compared to the clientele she'd expect to find at the Regal. "That's curious."

"That's why I want you on the scene. That fleabag in No-Man's-Land and the Regal are two different worlds, so it may just be an unfortunate coincidence. But I want your eyes on it to see if anything else matches up. The last thing the department needs for the holidays is a serial killer."

"Understood. I'll call in my team and get to the scene ASAP."

"The officers who responded to the call have blocked the door, so no one has been in there besides the maid that we know of. One of them will stay with the room, and the other will meet you in the lobby."

"That's good." Lexi jotted down the pertinent information the captain was giving her. "Did anyone at the hotel file a noise complaint about the fight? It might narrow down the time of death."

She heard a cheer from the crowd gathered at the police captain's house. Not only had the team they must be rooting for scored, but it sounded like there were plenty of friends and loved ones to share the excitement with. And while that observation triggered a surge of melancholic longing, Lexi quickly buried the emotion and listened to the rest of Captain Stockman's report. "There are a lot of parties going on in the city tonight. If anyone heard anything, they didn't report it. I've alerted Homicide and the ME's office," he added. "They can do a more thorough canvass of staff and guests. You focus on your job. Find us some clues."

"Yes, sir."

"I'll be out of the office until Monday. But call if you need anything. Good hunting."

"Thanks." Lexi tore off the paper with the information she needed and stuffed it into the pocket of her jeans. Then she grabbed her coat, kit, stocking cap and gloves, locked up her office and hurried down to the garage and CSIU van.

Lexi waved to the officer closing the garage door behind her and turned onto Brooklyn Avenue, heading south toward Thirty-Fifth Street. Before she reached the turn, she had Ethan Wynn on the line. "Hey, Ethan. Sorry to take you away from your girlfriend and the game, but we caught a DB down at the Regal Hotel."

"On the Plaza?"

"Yeah. It's one of the brownstone high-rises south of Brush Creek."

"I know where it is." Ethan seemed to be moving, gathering his gear or pulling on his coat, perhaps, while they talked. "It'll take me a while to get there with all the extra traffic in the area. And where are we going to park? Every spot on the streets for blocks in any direction will be taken."

She'd wondered that, too. "There's a lot behind the hotel."

"That'll be full."

"Well, if you can't get into the circular drive in front of the hotel, or the parking lot, do the best you can." The city road crews had done their job clearing snow off the streets, but since it was one of the busiest nights of the year for tourists and locals to pour into downtown KC, she was already running into a snarl of cars parked along every curb. "I'll call ahead to see if traffic patrol can clear a spot for us."

"Do you want me to drive to the lab and we can take the van together?"

She shook her head, as though he could see her through the phone she'd mounted on the dash. "I'm already en route. I want to get the scene taped off and under our control before the crowd on the Plaza breaks up and guests start coming back to their rooms at the Regal. Who knows what evidence all that extra foot traffic could contaminate for us. Plus, I'd like to at least get pictures of the place undisturbed before the detectives start their walk-through."

"I hear that." A door closed in the background, though whether it was him leaving his house or climbing into his car, she couldn't tell. "My kit's in the trunk. I'll drive straight to the crime scene and meet you there."

"Sounds good. And would you call Shane in, too? Captain Stockman said it's a mess. We can use the extra hands."

"Yes, ma'am. Will do. I'll see you there."

"Ma'am?" Was that sarcasm or a genuine attempt at humor? Was having her give the orders going to be a problem for Ethan? "Watch it, Wynn. You're older than me."

"Not by that much." He laughed. "It's the gray hair. Relax. I know today is your first day as the boss. I'm just practicing what I'm supposed to call you now."

"Well, knock it off. I'm still Lexi. Save your *ma'ams* for your grandmother."

"Yes, ma'am."

"Wise guy." She grinned and shook her head. "Thanks, Ethan. I'll start processing the scene. You and Shane get there as soon as you can."

What should have been about a twelve-minute drive stretched into twenty-five by the time Lexi pulled into the parking lot behind the Regal Hotel. Between KCPD and the hotel management, an area near the back entrance had been cleared for the official vehicles with flashing lights and law enforcement markings to be hidden away from public view to reduce the number of curious onlookers, press and potentially panicked guests who had no idea this luxury boutique hotel was now a crime scene.

There was another ten minutes of introducing herself to homicide detectives Keir Watson and Hud Kramer, who were just arriving on the scene, and listening to an initial report from Officer Olivo, who showed them upstairs to Room 920. She was glad to see the door was closed and yellow crime scene tape had been draped across the entrance to keep everyone out. Olivo's partner, Officer Heming, assured them no one had been in or out of the room since their arrival. Once dismissed, the two officers went to help the hotel's assistant manager move the other ninth-floor guests to a new location for the night.

"Booties, gentlemen." Lexi set her kit on the floor outside the crime scene and opened it up to retrieve foot coverings for the two detectives and herself. Since they had their own sterile gloves, she dropped her coat onto the carpet beside her kit, adjusted the CSI cap on her head and pulled on her gloves. Then she grabbed the flashlight and camera from her kit, reminded the officers not to touch the light switch until she could get it dusted, then swiped the key card and led the way into what had once been a beautifully appointed room.

It was a shambles now. A tabletop Christmas tree had been knocked to the floor, its glass ornaments shattered and strewn among crushed gift-wrapped boxes that had been stomped on or rolled over. There was an overturned chair and lamp. Pillows and bedding on the floor. A spilled bottle of champagne was soaking into the carpet. A dent and torn plaster in the wall that indicated where a fist or someone's head had hit.

A raven-haired woman lay sprawled on the floor in the middle of it all, her sightless eyes staring up at the ceiling. One of the victim's holly-shaped gold earrings, adorned with what Lexi guessed were real rubies, had been torn from her earlobe, and a length of drapery cord was cinched around her bruised neck.

Lexi sensed a lot of anger in this room. Had the victim been waiting for someone to celebrate Thanksgiving on the Plaza with her, but an intruder had broken in? Possibly an ex who was abusive and didn't like her hooking up with someone new? Or did she and her lover have a fight that had gotten out of hand and had ended with her dead on the floor and the room tossed as though there had been a real brawl here?

Detective Kramer, a compact, muscular man, seemed to have a flair for dark humor. "Happy holidays to her. I'm guessing the celebration didn't go the way she'd planned."

Detective Watson, wearing a suit and tie and long wool coat that were a dressy contrast to his partner's casual leather jacket and jeans, agreed. "I think we can safely assume this is a homicide."

After an initial look at the woman, who was probably about Lexi's age, Watson and Kramer asked Lexi to pull the victim's ID from her purse, which sat remarkably untouched on the bedside table. Lexi snapped a photograph of the purse before opening it. Jennifer Li was clearly expecting company, judging by the lacy underwear and silk robe she had on, as well as the expensive perfume still emanating from her skin. The drapes that hung at the bank of tall windows were all open, giving a spectacular view of the holiday lights down below.

Keir was studying the same open expanse. "I'm guessing at this height, none of those thousands of people out there saw anything."

"Unless the witness was flying by in a helicopter." Hud jotted the victim's information into a notebook and tucked it back into his pocket without touching anything in the room. He glanced at the contents of the wallet Lexi showed him, letting him see several credit cards and a stack of hundred-dollar bills. "I doubt this was a robbery if the perp left that much cash here."

Lexi agreed. "I wouldn't state anything conclusive, but I'm guessing we're looking at a crime of passion."

Hud thanked her before she replaced the wallet and retrieved a bag to drop the entire purse and its contents inside. "We'll back off and let you start processing the scene."

"I'll call my brother," Keir stated, following Hud back to the hallway. Was that code for something? Reading the question in her expression, Keir Watson explained, "My brother, Dr. Niall Watson, is the ME on call this weekend."

"Oh. Of course." Keir was younger than the bespectacled doctor she knew, but she could see the family resemblance now. "I've worked with Niall before."

Although the ME would determine the cause of death and collect any clues left on the body itself, Lexi could see that the woman had been strangled. Even without the cord around her neck, she'd recognized the dots of petechial hemorrhaging in and around Ms. Li's frozen eyes.

Keir was already halfway to the elevator, on his cell phone to his brother. Hud peeled off his booties while Lexi sealed and labeled the evidence bag with the victim's purse. "You'll be okay up here on your own?" he asked.

While Lexi appreciated the protective offer, she nodded. "I've got plenty to process in there."

"We're keeping Olivo downstairs to translate for the maid, and Heming's helping us make sure no one leaves the building until we get names and contact information on everyone. But if you'd feel more comfortable, I can send him back up here to keep an eye on you until the rest of your team arrives."

"I'll be fine on my own. I know you guys are short-staffed tonight, and the hotel is booked solid. Plus, with all the people coming and going with the holiday festivities, you'll need Heming for crowd control. The floor is clear, right?"

Hud nodded. "I'll run a double check myself before I leave you."

Keir ended his call and pushed the button to the elevator doors. "I'll head on down to the lobby to start the prelim interviews. We'll send your men up as soon as they arrive."

"Thanks."

Hud backed down the hallway in the opposite direction, starting his sweep of the ninth floor. "You'll coordinate with the ME and copy us on anything you find?"

"You bet."

She knew another cop and his K-9 partner who shared Hud Kramer's protective instincts. Lexi's thoughts strayed for a few moments, wondering how Aiden was spending his Thanksgiving. Although they saw each other nearly every day at work, they rarely spoke about their social lives. She had little interest in hearing about his latest conquest. Lexi knew Aiden dated—after all, what healthy, red-blooded woman could resist that sleeve of tats sliding over all those muscles, killer blue eyes and Irish charm? Although she would gladly face off against any woman who abused his feelings or took advantage of his generous, caring nature, she'd often wondered why he hadn't turned those charms on her. She supposed the pseudo-sibling bond was too strong between them for him to see her as anything but a little sister. And after her relationship with Kevin Nelson had blown up in her face, Aiden's hypercritical evaluations of anyone she tried to date made him seem more buttinsky brother than jealous lover when she talked about her social plans.

She imagined Aiden and Blue were in front of a televised football game with a pizza and a rawhide chew. She knew Aiden wouldn't be drinking beer and feeling sorry for himself at spending the holiday alone. His father had been an abusive alcoholic who'd married three different women after the death of Aiden's mother when he was just a baby. None of those marriages had lasted once his stepmothers realized they were either glorified babysitters or they became part of Patrick's abuse. Even after his father had lost his parental rights and eventually gone to jail, Aiden never touched alcohol. She didn't necessarily think that he believed the addiction was hereditary, but for as long as she'd known him, Aiden had avoided anything and anyone that could be remotely tied to the nightmarish memories he had of his childhood. He'd severed all ties with Patrick Murphy once her own parents had taken him in, both legally and emotionally.

For a moment, Lexi's heart ached for Aiden, as it always did. Unbidden came the admission that she ached for him in another way. The starving, broken boy she'd once known had grown into a strong, healthy, confident man. They shared such a close bond. And yet they would never share the bond she'd often fantasized about. Their friendship was too precious to risk, his vow to her brother too strong to betray.

All the men out there in the world, and she had to want the one who would never want her.

"Really, Callahan?" Lexi chided herself out loud at the dangerous turn her thoughts had taken. She was the one who was feeling sorry for herself. It happened every time that damn loneliness crept in. "He's probably a lousy kisser and leaves his dirty laundry all over the place. Probably forgets birthdays and anniversaries, too."

She tugged her knit cap tight around her hair and shook her head. She had no proof that any of that was true, but this pity party was only making the holiday and her first day as squad supervisor worse. She had a job to do. She needed to focus on that, and on helping find justice for poor Jennifer Li, not bemoaning her own foolish fantasies.

Lexi tucked a handful of marking labels into one of the pockets of her CSI utility vest and pushed to her feet. She ducked beneath the crime scene tape and took several pictures of the entire scene, working her way across the room to capture the general details from every angle. She paused at the window, feeling the cold from the air outside permeating the glass. She was glad she'd layered up with boots and a sweater. She could hear muffled bits of traffic noise and music from the world below her. So many lights. So much tradition. So many people.

It wasn't until Lexi turned and faced the room again that she shivered. She was alone with death and destruction while it looked like half the city was down on the Plaza celebrating the start of the Christmas season.

This was the job she was so good at, though, she had to remind herself. This was the work she loved. She was making a difference.

So she buried that crushing lonesomeness deep inside beside those useless feelings for Aiden Murphy and went back to work.

Lexi started at the broken tree and crushed gifts between the tall windows. She laid an evidence marker down beside the debris and snapped several pictures before picking up a package and reading the tag. "'To B, Love, J.'" She took a photo of the tag itself. None of the gifts had full names written on them. "Not particularly helpful, but it's a start." The detectives would need to track down whoever "B" was.

Then Lexi looked beyond the wreckage of a romantic holiday celebration and surveyed the chaos around the hotel suite. She'd better get a complete overview of the scene before she got caught up in the individual details. Steeling herself against the tragic loss of life, she snapped a few pictures of the body, including a close-up of the ligature around the victim's neck. She went back to the windows and searched beside each curtain until she found the one with the missing pull. She took a picture of that, too, and marked the rope for further investigation because it looked as though it had been cut with deliberation rather than torn from the window as a weapon of opportunity. Jackson Dobbs would be able to study the edge of the drapery pull and compare the cut pattern to his vast database of weaponry to determine what knife or other sharp instrument had been used to cut the cord.

Lexi watched her reflection in the window turn into a frown as a curious thought struck her. She slowly turned and scanned the room again. There were no sharp instruments here— no knives, no scissors, not even a letter opener. She turned her gaze to the open door of the adjoining bathroom. Would a pair of manicure scissors be heavy enough and sharp enough to cut the decorative cord? Jennifer Li seemed like a woman who cared enough about her appearance to pack a manicure set. But if manicure scissors were a weapon of opportunity—say the killer had dazed the victim enough to have the time to go cut the rope and then come back to strangle her—then how did he know where those scissors were? That indicated a very personal knowledge of the victim and her belongings. More likely, the killer had brought his own weapon. And that indicated premeditation. Both were significant possibilities that she needed to pass along to Detectives Watson and Kramer to explore further.

There was another possibility to this whole crime scene beyond the ideas of intimate knowledge of the victim or premeditation. It was one explanation for Jennifer Li's death she was hesitant to even give voice to.

Lexi scrolled through the pictures on her camera back to the crime scene she'd processed on Monday. The victim that night had been a prostitute found strangled to death in a rent-by-the-hour hotel over in the seedy No-Man's-Land district of KC, where drugs and street crime were king.

Although the victim, Giselle Byrd, had fresh heroin tracks in her arm rather than gold-and-ruby earrings, and the setting had been nothing like the classy sophistication of the Regal Hotel, there were other details that were the same. The room there had been tossed, indicating evidence of a major struggle. And the victim had been strangled with a length of cord from the curtains there. The setting and victimology didn't match at all. But the MO was the same.

Did they have a serial killer on their hands?

Lexi eased her breath out between pursed lips. No need to panic here. Her job was to collect and process evidence from the scene and present facts to the detectives working the case.

The emotional roller coaster she'd been on today—nerves at starting the new job, worries about changing friendships, forbidden thoughts about Aiden, this whole damn woe-is-me holiday thing that seemed to be hitting her extra hard this year—was affecting her ability to do her job. She was good at this because she *could* detach her emotions and stay focused on the task at hand. Observations about potential motives and crime scenarios were welcome; distractions that got in the way of doing her job were not.

With that resolve firmly in place again, Lexi became the supervising criminalist she was meant to be. She sent quick texts to Ethan and Shane, informing them that she was at the scene and had started processing. She warned them it would probably be a long night. When they got there, she'd divide the suite into grids and put them to work collecting and cataloging the extensive evidence without overwhelming any of them.

She received a quick thumbs-up from Shane and another Yes, ma'am from Ethan with a winking emoji. Lexi snickered at his immature stab at humor and tucked her phone into the back pocket of her jeans.

Just in case she could find a pair of manicure scissors or other sharp object for Jackson to compare to the cut marks on the drapery cord, Lexi moved her assessment into the adjoining bathroom. She mentally swore when she saw that the fight must have continued in here, too.

There were bloody fingerprints on the edge of the porcelain sink and chrome faucet. A larger pool of blood was smeared inside the sink and trickled down the drain. She'd sure like Grayson Malone's opinion here. He'd be able to tell her if this was from the killer cleaning up, or from the victim, trying to doctor her own wounds before she expired. But since Gray wasn't here, Lexi documented it all on her camera, then swabbed several samples and bagged and tagged them for Grayson to analyze in the lab.

Lexi closed the swab she'd taken from the sink trap and was labeling the plastic tube when she heard a whisper of sound from the main room. She paused where she knelt on the cold tile floor and listened for some other indicator that she had company. "Hello?"

When she got no reply, she wondered if the sound had come from the floor above or below her. She tucked the tube inside her kit next to the cubby where she'd stowed her camera and tried to pinpoint the source of the sound. She likened the soft, rustling noise to the sound of someone who was slightly winded—as if they'd just walked up a flight of stairs because the elevator to the ninth floor had been shut down until the medical examiner removed the body and the police cleared the scene.

Lexi released the breath she didn't realize she'd been holding and opened another swab tube to collect a blood sample from the floor. "Ethan? Shane? I'm in here."

When she still got no response, she stopped working. Her imagination wasn't so fanciful to imagine that Jennifer Li had sat up in the next room. Maybe Detective Watson had sent the uniformed officer back upstairs for some reason. "Officer Heming? Is that you?" No answer. "Detective Watson? Detective Kramer?"

Damn it. Either someone had an extreme case of rudeness, they were playing a practical joke she didn't find particularly funny, or she had an intruder. Even if one of the guests had peeked into the room or, heaven forbid, a reporter had gotten past the police downstairs to take a picture, it was Lexi's responsibility to get rid of that person before they contaminated her crime scene.

Pulling the lanyard with her ID card from inside her vest, she got up and headed into the main room. "I need you to identify yourself. I'm Supervisor Callahan with the Kansas City Police Department Crime Lab. You can't be in here…"

There was no one in the room. No one hovering in the doorway.

But the drapes had been closed.

A chill of fear raised the tiny hairs at the nape of her neck and shuddered down her spine.

A spike of adrenaline followed quickly in its wake.

She had company.

Not wasting another moment, she made a quick sweep of the room. Dead body. Major struggle. Ruined holiday. All the same, except for the damn curtains.

Lexi pulled her phone from her jeans and punched in Ethan Wynn's number as she stepped outside of the room and scanned up and down the hallway. No sign of her team. No Officer Heming. No one.

When that call went to voice mail, she disconnected and called Shane Duvall. She snapped into the phone the moment Shane picked up. "Where are you guys?"

"Well, hello to you, too. I'm stuck in traffic."

"What's your ETA?"

"I'm *stuck*." His tone indicated he wanted to add a "duh" onto the end of that sentence.

But something was off enough that it was giving her the creeps, and she didn't appreciate his sarcasm at the moment. "Did Ethan call you? You know to come to Room 920?"

"Of course. Ethan's not there yet? He's probably stuck in this traffic mess, too."

"Get here as soon as you can, okay?"

"Lexi, is everything—?"

But she had already disconnected and was scrolling through the numbers on her phone. She needed backup.

She went straight to the *A*s and pressed the familiar number.

"Lex!" When Aiden picked up, he launched into a silly, friendly chat. "I know you're calling to invite me to Black Friday dinner since we both pulled shifts on Thanksgiving. I may have the bigger TV to watch football, but you're the better cook. And I know my priorities—"

"Aiden. Stop talking. Something's wrong."

The teasing ended abruptly. "Talk to me." He was all serious. All cop. All the protector she could ever ask for. "Lex?"

She slowly turned 360 degrees, scanning for any sign of movement, any door standing ajar, any sound of labored breathing she might not have imagined. "I'm at the Regal Hotel. Processing a murder in Room 920."

She heard the instant response of the siren on his truck suddenly piercing the sounds of traffic in the background. She explained the creep factor and feeling she wasn't alone, even though there was no one here but the dead body.

"Get out of there," Aiden ordered. She heard Blue whining in the background, probably picking up on his partner's alertness and the sound and speed of the two of them heading into action. "Tape it off and go back down to the lobby, where there are people. Send the officers up to recheck the scene. Go now. I'll be there in five minutes."

Five minutes? She could do five minutes.

"Move, Lex. Now!"

Lexi couldn't leave her kit unattended now that she'd cataloged evidence. She disconnected the call, hurried back to the bathroom, snapped it shut and ran for the door.

Five minutes would be too late.

The moment she set foot in the hallway again, a fist smashed against her cheekbone, knocking her into the doorjamb. As pain rang through her skull, her kit hit the floor and tumbled into the opposite wall. Before she could even think to fight or run, the leather-gloved hand palmed her face and smacked the back of her head into the steel door frame. She crumpled to the floor, tried to crawl, but her attacker grabbed the collar of her vest and sweater to pull her up and toss her into the room, where she landed hard, stinging her breasts and hip.

She tasted the coppery taint of blood in her mouth. It seemed she could literally hear ball bearings clanging around in her skull. Her stomach churned as she turned her head and got a glimpse of black swirling through her vision. Black pants. Black gloves. Black mask hiding the man's features. It had to be a man, didn't it? To pick her up like that?

Was this Jennifer Li's killer? Returning to the scene of the crime?

Thinking she was down for the count, the attacker walked past her, intent on reaching something else in the room. Lexi rolled onto her side and kicked out. Her legs tangled with his, tripping him. She pushed herself up and kicked again, connecting with his knee and sending him sprawling. She rolled to her feet and staggered toward escape. But landing a blow only elicited a feral growl from her attacker.

Lexi lurched toward the door. But the man recovered faster. He grabbed a fistful of her hair and smashed her face into the wall until her knees buckled. The ball bearings went silent and the world faded to black.

Chapter Four

"Blue takes point." Aiden raised his fist, halting the contingent of police officers and detectives waiting behind him on the landing of the ninth-floor stairwell. "Come on, boy." He rubbed Blue around the ears and patted the flanks of the black protective vest the dog wore, getting the highly motivated, super focused Malinois vibrating with excitement and fired up to go to work. "You know you want to do this. You know you want to find the bad guy." The moment he felt the fierce tug against his arm, Aiden nodded to the officer who swiped a key card to open the door. Aiden unhooked Blue's leash. "Go get him!"

The muscular dog leaped into the hallway, put his nose to the carpet and systematically touched every doorway, including the elevators. Aiden moved out right behind him with his gun drawn and clasped squarely between both hands. He looked first to the far end of the hallway to ensure there was no one in the passageway itself. "Clear!"

Officers Heming and Olivo, followed by Detectives Watson and Kramer, were all on his hit list right now for leaving Lexi alone at the crime scene, especially when he'd stormed in downstairs, asked if she was all right, and they had no idea what he was talking about. But he was glad to have them at his back now as they split to check each door in the hallway to ensure that it was locked. Blue worked at twice their pace, sniffing every door and circling back by the time Aiden reached 920. The door stood slightly ajar behind the crisscross of yellow crime scene tape, and it was the only one that Blue paused at. He whined with anticipation, indicating he detected the scent of a human inside.

"I've got a hit," Aiden informed the others. He ordered Blue into a sit, then leaned in, but saw nothing more than shadows through the half-inch opening of the door. He quieted his breathing and trained his ears toward any sounds coming from inside.

There. A soft moan. A grunt of pain? There was definitely someone alive in there. But was it Lexi? Or something he couldn't allow himself to imagine?

"Elevator's still locked out," Watson reported, jogging up beside him. "Nobody came in that way. Heming? Olivo? You split up and search the floors above and below. If you run into anyone who can't prove they're staff or a guest, I want to meet them downstairs."

"Yes, sir."

"Yes, sir."

"This is your call, Murphy." Watson took up a support position behind Aiden while Kramer flattened his back on the wall beside the door.

The open CSI kit that lay overturned and spilled on the carpet was not a good sign. When Blue dropped his nose to the vials, brushes and camera, Aiden pulled the dog's attention back to him. "Leave it."

Blue was panting hard, more from excitement than exertion. This was all a game to him, and he hadn't found the intruder he was looking for yet. And until he found the person that his handler wanted him to flush out, the game wouldn't be over. He wouldn't get Aiden's praise or the chance to play with his Kong until he won the game.

His dark eyes were focused up on Aiden, waiting, waiting, waiting…

Aiden switched the gun to his left hand and wrapped his fingers around the doorknob. He winked down at Blue. Still waiting… "KCPD! Come out now, or I'm sending a K-9 in," Aiden warned. Silence. "Your choice. I'm sending in the dog." He pushed the door open just enough for the Malinois's shoulders to pass through, and Blue charged. "Find the bad guy!"

A few seconds later, Blue's black muzzle reappeared in the doorway and Aiden pushed the door wide open, knowing it was safe. He wanted to swear at the scene that greeted him. Instead, he wrestled the dog around his face and neck and praised him for completing the job. "Good boy. Good boy, Blue. You da man."

Watson and Kramer streamed in behind them, one checking the bathroom, the other the closet and under the bed. "Clear!"

"Clear!"

Aiden holstered his weapon and pulled out the hard red rubber Kong that Blue adored and tossed it into the hallway. Instead of chasing after his reward, the dog trotted beside Aiden as he hurried to the woman with the short golden-brown hair that clung to her face. Lexi was on the floor at the foot of the bed, trying to get her arms beneath her to push herself up.

"Bwue?" Her eyes were squeezed shut. No, one was nearly swollen shut and the other was squinting against the light as she gingerly plopped onto her back and reached out to touch Blue's chest. "Knew…you'd come." She wrapped her fingers through the dog's collar and tried to pull herself up.

This time Aiden made no apology for swearing as he knelt beside her. "Don't move, Lex." He gently cupped her shoulders and eased her back to the carpet. "We don't know how badly you're hurt. Internal injuries? Your neck?" He pulled off his glove and stroked her staticky hair away from the blood pooling beneath her nose and from the split in her bottom lip. He stroked the cheek beneath her unbruised eye again, hating the chill he felt there. He turned his head to his shoulder without losing sight of her narrowed eyes. "Call a medic. Officer down."

Keir Watson strode out into the hallway, making the call on his phone while Hud Kramer took up space in the doorway, the way someone should have been to keep this assault from happening in the first place. He was making a separate call to his Fourth Precinct office, asking for any available backup at the hotel. Without any command, Blue stretched out on the carpet beside Lexi. She slid her hand along the dog's back, perhaps taking comfort in the dog's presence, perhaps absorbing some of Blue's abundant warmth.

"Aiden?" She blinked her good eye open, then squinted as though even the lone light shining in from the bathroom caused her pain.

"Shh, Lex. I'm right here." He shifted his position beside her to block the light, then reached across her to pet Blue and praise him for remaining surprisingly still at his post. "Help's on the way."

He made a visual assessment of her injuries. He'd been in enough fights growing up to recognize the imprint of a fist on her cheek. Bruises were forming quickly on the thinner skin around her face. The cut that was oozing blood in her hairline was sprinkled with plaster. He made a quick visual sweep around the room and spotted the broken dents and droplets of blood in the wall near the door. Yeah, he'd had those injuries, too. But it was tearing him up inside to see that Lexi had suffered this kind of a beating, to know the pain she was suffering, to understand that helpless feeling of not knowing when the next blow would come.

"Can you tell me what happened?" he asked.

Although she seemed to have a death grip on Blue's vest, her right hand tapped at Aiden's thigh and stomach. Then he realized she was trying to find his hand. He completed the connection for her and felt a tad of relief at the strength of her grip in his. She inhaled a deep breath, probably a good sign that she didn't have any cracked or broken ribs. "I was on my way downstairs, like you said. I didn't see him. In the hallway. One minute he wasn't there, and then he was. He hit me, and… I couldn't fight back. I tried. I couldn't get away. I guess I passed out." Her eyes shut and a tear squeezed out, and that tore him up more than the cuts and scrapes and bruises did. "I tripped him once. Got in a good kick, so he may be limping for a while. But I couldn't get away. The self-defense training you and Levi taught me didn't do me a damn bit of good."

He tugged his other glove off between his

teeth and dropped it to the floor beside him, then reached down to gently capture that tear with the pad of his thumb and wipe it away. "It's practically impossible to defend yourself against a blitz attack."

"I don't even know what he wanted." Her grip pulsed around his. "He never said anything."

"A killer returning to the scene of his crime?" He didn't have to spell out the obvious. He'd come back for something, an incriminating piece of evidence, most likely, and had found Lexi here, standing between him and what he wanted. He'd needed her out of commission so he could retrieve whatever he was after.

"Is anything missing?" Lexi suspected the same thing. "I need to look. Help me." She pulled against his hand, trying to sit up despite his warning. Twisting her head around, she surveyed the room, moaning at even that slight movement. "My head feels like a bowling ball, rolling toward the pins."

"I told you not to move." With her visible injuries, and uncertain hidden injuries, Aiden wasn't about to wrestle her back to the floor. Instead, he sat on the carpet, pulling her halfway into his lap so that she could lean back against his chest. It wasn't any kind of defensible position if the perp returned, but if using him as a backboard would keep her relatively still until the paramedics got here, then he'd stay put.

The crown of her head lolled back against his neck, and he wrapped his arm lightly around her waist to anchor her in place. "The whole room is spinning. And it's cold." He released her hand and snugged his arms more tightly around her, trying to share the body heat she needed. She lifted her fingers to her hair, becoming aware of the extent of her injuries. Or not. "Where's my stocking cap?"

Maybe she wanted it for warmth. He surveyed the scene again, looking for the familiar cap that usually hugged her golden-brown waves. "I don't see it. Blue." At his subtle hand gesture, the dog moved in beside her again, resting his muzzle atop her thigh, adding his abundant heat. She rewarded him by stroking his head and jowl. Player. It seemed the beast got more affection from Lexi than he did. But Lexi was a beloved part of the dog's pack, and Blue snuggled up to her without any hesitation, much like they practiced with the dog lying beside Aiden to protect him should he ever be injured in the line of duty.

Lexi tipped her head slowly from side to side, searching the room the best she could with one good eye and punctuating each turn with a hushed little gasp or groan. Although her blood dripped onto the sleeve of his jacket, Aiden kept her anchored against him to minimize her movement and keep her from aggravating her injuries. He turned his gaze to the compact detective in the doorway the moment Hud Kramer ended his call. "Where the hell is her team? Why did you leave her alone?"

Hud squared his shoulders against the accusation. "She said she had this. Entry points were secured. I cleared the floor myself. Trust me, the perp wouldn't have gotten anywhere near her if I'd known he still had access to the floor."

Lexi's fingers tightened around his hand. "Take a breath, Aiden. It's not their fault."

"It sure as hell is somebody's fault."

"What happened to my stocking cap?" She must have taken a good blow to the head to be obsessing about that and not her injuries. "It was probably enough cushion to keep my skull from cracking open, but now I don't see it anywhere."

Aiden dutifully swept the room again, but he still didn't see the knit cap with *CSI* embroidered on the front. He reached up and tugged the black knit cap from his own head. "Here. If you're cold, wear mine."

He released her hand to pull the cap over the top of her head, but she suddenly stiffened against him and knocked his hand away. "Wait! Don't touch anything!" She hunched away from him, as if his chest suddenly scorched her. "Don't touch me."

"Lex—"

"There may be evidence on me." She wobbled, fighting to stay upright without his support.

"Huh?"

"*I'm* a crime scene!"

Aiden pulled his cap down over her hair, hopefully locking in some of his body heat. Then he slipped off his insulated jacket. God, she was shaky and looked so pale. "Right now, you're a crime scene who's going into shock."

"I want to process my clothes. He could have left trace on me."

She made a token effort to fight with him, but even if she was 100 percent, he was stronger, and whether she liked it or not, he was in full-on protector mode. He understood that she was all about the job, but right now, he was all about her. He gently wrapped his jacket around her shoulders and snapped it together at the collar. "My jacket will preserve any evidence that's already on you. You can keep it and process it. I've got a spare in my truck."

With the softest of nods, she seemed to calm at his suggestion. She eyed the sterile gloves covering her hands after she pushed them through the sleeves. "There won't be any scrapings under my nails." She pointed to her foot on the floor beside his. "I kicked him. I may have picked up fibers off his clothes. I need to preserve that..." Her head was still bobbing from side to side, although she was leaning against him again, that burst of protest having expended what was left of her energy. "Where's the bootie I was wearing? He had on gloves. But he might have injured himself. Lots of scrapes in a fight. There has to be trace. I just have to find it." Her thoughts bombarded from one observation to the next, making it difficult to follow her conversation. He hoped this was her detail-oriented brain kicking in, sussing out possible clues, and not some rambling side effect of the blows to her head. She reached back to palm the curve of her hip. "My phone's missing. Why would he take…?" Her frantic, disconnected movements suddenly stopped when her focus landed on the dead body lying a few feet away. "Oh, my God. Jennifer…"

"The victim?"

Aiden felt the fight in Lexi try to reassert itself. His pulse leaped as she braced a hand against his thigh, and she pushed herself toward the body. Digging her fingers into his leg to anchor herself, she stretched out her other arm across Blue, reaching for the dark-haired woman. Lexi's fingers danced around the woman's earlobe without touching the body. "He took her earring. Gold and rubies. And the cord around her throat. The probable murder weapon…" Lexi collapsed between Aiden's legs again, the brief burst of emotional adrenaline giving way to her injuries. "He stole evidence. This whole case has been tainted."

"Don't get yourself so worked up. We've still got the body. Doc Watson is bound to find something."

"*I'm* supposed to find something useful."

"And you will. Just not until we get you checked out." He glanced back at the detective guarding the doorway. "Can we get a cool washcloth out of the john?"

"No." Lexi stopped Kramer before he got two steps into the room. "No one else comes in until my team can assess the damage that guy did."

Aiden bit down on his frustration with her putting the case above her own needs. "Either of you got anything I can stanch this cut with?"

Detective Watson stepped up behind his partner and tossed Aiden a white handkerchief. "Here. Ambulance is downstairs. The assistant manager is unlocking the elevator to send them up. One of your team is on his way up, too."

"Finally." Aiden caught the folded square of cotton and shook it loose from its neat folds to gently press it against Lexi's forehead to keep the blood from running into her swollen eye. "Easy, Lex." When she opened her mouth to protest, he silenced her with some of her own logic. "You don't want to drip blood on your crime scene, do you?" Aiden tucked the wadded cotton underneath the knit cap to hold it in place. "How did the perp get by the guards at the elevator and stairwells?"

Keir Watson pulled back the front of his coat and propped his hands at his waist. "Must have been in a room on another floor. Or a service hallway we don't know about. He was in the building the whole time, hiding out somewhere. He must have been moving ahead of our sweep. He'd need to have a master access key to get through the doors."

Aiden was aware of Lexi still turning, even as she leaned against him, to study the mess around them as he and the detectives tried to make sense of what had happened. "You think someone on staff is responsible for this?" He wasn't talking about the murder, although surely the dead woman and the attack on Lexi were linked.

Watson shook his head. "Not necessarily. The guests' key cards work on the stairwell doors, too."

"Somebody could have swiped one," Hud Kramer added. "So this guy was hiding out, waiting for his chance to get back to the crime scene and remove whatever evidence would have incriminated him."

But Lexi didn't intend to be left out of the conversation. "Guys, I was only alone for maybe thirty minutes."

Aiden checked his watch. "You called me fifteen minutes ago." His gaze zeroed in on the detectives. "That means the attack and theft happened in that narrow time frame."

Hud glanced up at his partner, realization dawning on each of them. "He's still in the building."

Keir pulled out the phone he seemed to live by and called someone for a sit rep. "He couldn't have gotten out. We still have every outside exit blocked."

Blue whined at the sudden alertness surging through Aiden. "Unless this was a diversion to get everyone away from their posts so he *could* get out."

Lexi tugged at Aiden's arm. "He stole evidence. Jennifer Li's investigation has been compromised. You have to find this guy before he can destroy the things he took. The murder weapon."

Keir exchanged a nod with his partner. "Floor-by-floor search. Now."

"We're on it. If we can't find him, then maybe we can find his hiding place." As Hud was backing out, he pointed to Lexi. "You'll stay with her?"

"I'm not going anywhere."

"Keep us posted."

Once Aiden was alone with Lexi and Blue and the body, he thought she'd relax. Instead, he felt her pushing against him again. "If they're searching the building, they need you and Blue. I'll be fine. You go."

"Not gonna happen."

"I'm keeping you from doing your job," she argued.

"Part of our job is to protect the members of the CSIU. You called me for backup, and here I am. I only wish Blue and I had gotten here a few minutes sooner."

After the slightest of nods, she burrowed into his chest again. For a split second the lines between protecting Levi's sister and holding the woman he cared far too much about blurred.

But Lexi never forgot that she'd come here to work. She was staring at the windows, that battered brain of hers still searching for answers. "Why did he close the drapes?"

Aiden glanced out at the night sky, warmed by the glow of lights from the Plaza, even at this height. "They're not closed."

"They were open when I started. Then he closed them. That's how I knew something was wrong."

"Maybe he just didn't want anyone seeing that he'd returned to the scene of the crime."

"But why open them again? There has to be a reason." She collapsed inside Aiden's jacket, her chin resting on the collar, her grip on his hand weakening. Where were those medics?

Aiden heard another man's voice, exchanging a quick greeting with Watson and Kramer. "Hey, Detective. I got here as soon as I could. Came up the stairs like you said… Oh. Okay. They're in a hurry." The bearded criminalist with the glasses who reminded Aiden of a stodgy college professor appeared in the doorway. "Lexi? What happened?"

"Shane." Lexi sat up and lifted her chin as

though the movement wouldn't rattle the ball bearings in her skull. "Thank God."

"You're hurt." His initial surprise seemed to be the extent of his emotional reaction to seeing his coworker bruised and bloody at a murder scene. The criminalist pushed his glasses up onto the bridge of his nose and looked around the room. Like Lexi, Shane Duvall was a stickler for details. He opened his kit and slipped on his booties and gloves out in the hallway before entering the room. "What happened?"

Was everyone going to try his patience here tonight? "Someone assaulted her while she was working the scene. Where have you been?"

Duvall's gaze turned to Aiden as if he hadn't realized there was an armed cop sitting behind Lexi and holding her upright. "My son and I spent the day at my parents' in Lee's Summit with the rest of the family. We were on the way home when Ethan called. I had to turn around and drive him back so they could watch him before I came here. He's only two."

"Then you leave him with his mother."

Lexi's grip pulsed around his. A warning?

"His mother is dead," Duvall stated matter-of-factly.

Aiden was upset about so many people dropping the ball with Lexi's safety, but he didn't mean to be a complete jerk. "Oh, man. I'm sorry."

If Duvall took offense at the insensitive remark, he didn't show it. "I do need to look into hiring someone to be with him full-time when I'm on call. That makes sense."

"Lexi getting hurt doesn't make any sense."

"Hey," Lexi chided, turning halfway around to face Aiden. "Ease up. He's part of my team, not yours." The hand resting against his chest and curling into the edge of his protective vest eased the sting of her reprimand. "Shane does logic-speak. He doesn't have an Irish temper like you. Yelling at him won't help him understand."

Shane carried his kit into the room. "It's okay. I'd be pissy, too, if my girl got hurt. If I had a girl-friend."

Her fingers still clung to him, belying her words. "Oh, I'm not his—"

"Where's the rest of your team?" Aiden inter-rupted, not wanting to put a name to the emotion flaring inside at hearing how quick Lexi was to deny even the possibility they could be more than friends. "I know it's the holiday, but she could have been killed."

"Aiden!"

He wasn't glossing over the extent of what had happened here. "Honey, you can't see your face the way I can. Your words are slurring from the swelling in your lip. That cut on your head needs stitches. You won't stop working and lie still. Where the hell's that medic?"

She frowned. "Honey?"

Oh, man, he was slipping badly here.

Blue rolled to his paws at the ding of the elevator and hurried footsteps of a man jogging through the hallway. "Lexi! Lexi?"

"Easy, boy," Aiden warned, urging the dog into a sit when he recognized the voice. "In here, Wynn."

Although Ethan Wynn was close to Aiden's age, his graying hair made him seem older. He stopped in the doorway and made a quick sweep of the hotel suite. Then he zeroed in on Lexi in the middle of all of it and let out a low whistle. "The cop at the back door said I needed to get up here pronto. You look like you got hit by a truck."

Lexi stirred against Aiden's chest. "You here to work or pay me compliments?"

"Sarcasm is intact." Wynn grinned at Lexi's barb. "She's going to be okay."

Shane gestured to Ethan to put on his protective gear before entering the room. Then he turned to Lexi. "What do you need from us?"

"Take the drapes and cords with us. There was a ligature around the victim's neck the perp came back for. Maybe we can match fibers or the bruising pattern to the drapery cord." She paused to draw in a deep breath, but Aiden hated what this show of strength was costing her. "The guy who attacked me was wearing gloves, so you won't find prints. But we can check for trace. Fibers. Anything he tracked in."

"On it, boss."

"I've processed the bathroom already. Divide the main room into grids and get through it as quickly as you can. I'll download the preliminary pics from my camera, and we can compare if anything besides the earring and ligature are missing or have been tampered with." She paused to press at the handkerchief wadded against her forehead. "Oh, and see if you can find my phone and stocking cap."

"Roger that." Shane immediately went to work.

Ethan got nudged out of the hallway by two paramedics and the gurney they set up across from the open doorway. With one bootie on and one yet in his hand, he hopped on one foot, whisking on the other foot covering before stumbling into the room. "Ouch," he joked at having to catch himself on the chair beside the door. He sat down on it to finish his prep. "Lots of casualties here. This room must be jinxed."

Before Aiden could comment on his tactless dark humor, Lexi growled an order. "Get to work, Ethan."

"I'm gettin' there." He pushed to his feet. "Don't you worry about a thing except getting to the hospital. Shane and I can handle this."

"Phone!" Shane announced, holding up the cell he'd pulled from under the bed. He knelt in front of her. "Here."

Lexi snatched her hands back from the offering. "No. Bag it. I don't remember it falling out of my pocket. I want to dust it for prints, just in case he tampered with it."

With a nod, Duvall went to his kit to do her bidding.

When she saw the first EMT duck beneath the tape, she warned them away. "Stay out! I'll come to you." She braced her hand against Aiden's shoulder and struggled to get her feet beneath her and stand. He could tell the room must be spinning. She squeezed her good eye shut and dropped her forehead against his collar. "Too many people in the room. This scene has been contaminated enough already."

"Ma'am, you shouldn't move. Let us do the prelim—"

"No," she muttered under her breath. "I've already screwed this up enough. First damn day in charge…" Enough. Aiden got to his knees and scooped Lexi up into his arms. Her head stayed where it was, nestled against his collar. But her fingers latched on to his neck and shoulder as he lifted her against his chest and stood. "What are you doing?"

"You need to see the medic. If you won't let them come to you, I'm taking you to them."

"You're not the boss of me, Aiden Murphy."

Well, if that line wasn't a blast from their childhood? He smiled. "Tonight, I am. Blue! *Fuss.*" He ordered the dog to follow them into the hallway, out of the way of the criminalists now working the scene. He set Lexi on the gurney, laying her back against the pillow as the lead medic stepped in to check her vitals and pupil reaction. A second medic nudged Aiden aside to cover Lexi with a blanket and hook up an IV. She didn't protest when he peeled off her glove and inserted the needle into the back of her hand. "Hang in there, Lex. Let them do their job."

Shane brought the bagged and tagged phone out to Lexi, and she tucked it into the pocket of the jacket she was still wearing. The female medic with long auburn hair grilled Lexi with several questions while she removed the soiled handkerchief, debrided the wound, then packed it with sterile gauze before sliding the knit cap back into place. Good. Aiden liked that Lexi was surrounded by his cap and jacket since he couldn't get to her right now.

The redhead seemed satisfied with her examination and pulled up the rails on the gurney. "What's the verdict?" Lexi asked.

"Probable concussion." While the second EMT packed their med kit and set it on the foot of the gurney, the redhead checked the IV drip and gently slid an ice pack against the knot on Lexi's scalp. "I don't think anything's broken, but I can't give you anything for the pain until the doctors check you out."

"I don't want anything. I'm already fuzzy

enough." His jacket swallowed her up as she huddled beneath the blanket. "Did someone open a window? Why is it so cold?"

"We set up some IV fluids to rebuild your blood volume and keep you from going into shock."

"Here." Aiden was having a hard time standing back and doing nothing. But he spotted Lexi's own coat on the floor and spread it on top of her. "Better?"

She nodded slightly. But when he moved to step out of the way, she pulled her hand from beneath the layers of warmth and reached for him. Aiden grabbed on and didn't let go as the EMTs rolled the gurney onto the elevator. With Blue at his side, Aiden rode down to the main lobby and walked with them outside to the ambulance. He thought with the bite of cold air, she'd withdraw and snuggle under the covers again. But Lexi's grip never once let up.

Even when they reached the back of the ambulance itself, and the medics gave them a couple of minutes while they stowed their gear, Lexi held his hand. Maybe she needed the reassurance of that connection as much as he did.

"I feel like I've been in a prizefight," she confessed.

He wasn't going to tell her she looked it, too. How was he going to explain this to Levi? He had one job to do while his best friend was deployed, and he'd failed miserably. He wasn't failing again. If he and Blue had to work around the clock, he was going to find out who had hurt Lexi, and he wouldn't let that SOB get anywhere close to her again. Then maybe he could look Levi in the eye and tell him he'd done right by the Callahan family. Then maybe that fist of anger, fear and potential loss that was choking his heart would ease its grip and let him go back to being good ol' Aiden Murphy, annoying big brother and friend.

When he couldn't come up with a *"You'll be fine"*, she started relaying directions for her team again. "Tell Shane and Ethan to check all the doors on the ninth floor. See if any of the locks have been jimmied, or if there's residue from being taped off to keep the security locks from engaging. I need to call Chelsea in to run through the hotel's computer system, see if there were any anomalous key swipes recorded. And someone needs to pack up my kit and bring it to the hospital. I want to bag the clothes I'm wearing before anything happens to them."

"They'll figure it out, Lex. No one on your team is a rookie."

"They need direction. I'm their supervisor."

"Right now, you're a patient. Your brain has already been beat up enough tonight, okay? It needs to rest."

"But—"

"Damn it, Lex. When my dad used to wallop me, the school nurse said I needed to lie still and give my body a chance to heal itself." His breath gusted out into a white cloud in the cold air between them.

When the cloud cleared, he saw the stricken look he'd put on her face. She brushed her fingertips against her split lip and bruised eye. "I'm sorry. Does what happened to me remind you of him? I shouldn't have asked you to come."

"You absolutely should have." Aiden bit down on a curse. Because his emotions were so screwed up, he was causing the very stress in Lexi he was trying to help her avoid. "Patrick Murphy is old history. *Very* old history. I was just a boy then." She knew the kind of training he did. Lifting weights. Sparring in the gym. Running with Blue. "I'd like to see him come after me now."

Her fingers slid up his sleeve to squeeze the muscles in his forearm. "Poor Patrick."

He covered her hand with his where it rested on his arm. "I'm just saying I've got experience with this sort of thing. You need to stop being a criminalist for thirty seconds, and let the medics take care of you. You need to rest."

"Okay." It scared him even more that she capitulated so quickly once he'd made the argument personal. He was used to her challenging him, asserting herself as his equal, not worrying about the old hurts and resentments he'd left in his past. "I'll do what they say. For a little while." The corner of her mouth curved into a weak smile, and he felt even more like a heel for causing her one whit of concern about him. "I'll be fine. Don't you worry about me."

"Blue!" The dog trotted up beside him. Aiden hooked him up to his leash. "I'm going with you to the hospital. I'll drive ahead of you and clear traffic with my truck."

"No, you won't. If KCPD is doing a room-to-room search, they need you and Blue here. They're already short-staffed, and Blue does the work of several men."

"*You're* my priority."

"Because Levi said so?" She pulled away with a weary sigh, tucking her hand back under the blanket. "I know the promise you made to him to take care of me while he's overseas. But I am not going to be a burden to him or you or anybody. You have a job to do. Just like I did. Let's not screw anything else up because of me."

Aiden was struggling between duty and his feelings for her. "Sure, I made a promise to Levi. I want to always do right by the Callahan family." He realized he'd left his gloves up at the crime scene, so he stuffed his fingers into the pockets of his black BDU pants and hunched his shoulders against the cold. "Tonight, I let him down. I let you both down."

"Aiden—"

"I could have lost you tonight. I don't want to let you out of my sight."

"I'll be in an ambulance with the paramedics. Then I'll be in the hospital with hundreds of other people. I won't be alone."

"There are hundreds of people here at this hotel tonight, and you were still alone."

She flinched as though his words had dealt her another blow. She looked away at the emergency lights swirling through the crowd of onlookers gathering on the far side of the iron fence surrounding the hotel's front drive. When she turned her face back to his, her brave, bruised smile was back in place. "Go. Do your job. One of us needs to. Right now, I have to be the patient, right? So you go be the cop."

"Look at you, being all smart and throwing my words back at me." He touched a short strand of silky hair peeking out from the edge of the cap and stroked it back into place behind her ear. "You're not a burden to me, Lex. Not ever. You're…"

"Family?"

Sure. He'd go with that.

The red-haired EMT interrupted their conversation. "We need to go, sir."

Aiden nodded and pulled away as the medics

loaded the gurney into the back of the ambulance. "You'll do what they say?"

"I'll be fine."

"Not what I asked, Callahan."

The ambulance doors started to close. That felt like shutting him out, like no matter what he did, he'd always be on the outside, looking in on Lexi's world.

"Aiden?"

He grabbed the door before it closed, always ready to answer her call.

She had her hand outstretched, reaching for him. And when he climbed into the back to take her hand, the EMT discreetly stepped back so that he could kneel beside her. "What do you need?"

"Forget about Levi and make a promise to me tonight."

"Anything."

"Go. Find this guy. Or find me some evidence so I can track him down." That promise went without saying. "But when you're done here, could you come by the hospital? No matter how late it is? I'll need a ride home."

He nodded to the uncertainty dulling those beautiful green eyes. She wasn't worried about a ride. She was asking for backup. Even though this one-sided relationship that could never be was eating him up inside, Aiden would never say no if she needed him. He leaned in and brushed a gentle kiss across the least bruised part of her face he could find.

When he pulled back, he winked. "Count on it."

Chapter Five

"Here you go." The blonde nurse set the plastic bag filled with medical supply trash in Lexi's lap. "It's an odd request, but I bagged everything we used on you except for the hypodermic. All the swabs and gauze are there. Sealed and labeled it myself like you said."

"Thank you."

"It felt like we were putting together a rape kit on you, swabbing all your injuries." Her forehead knit together in a gentle frown. "Are you sure you weren't sexually assaulted and want us to do a full kit?"

"Thank you for being concerned, but no." Lexi waved her hand around her face. "I'm certain all the injuries are up here. Thank you for being so thorough."

"Glad I could help. Take it easy until your ride gets here." While Lexi tucked the bag on the hospital bed beside her, the nurse set the call button on her pillow. "Even though we're not admitting you, if you start to feel woozy, you need help getting dressed or anything else, just push that button."

As soon as the nurse left the semiprivate room off the ER where Lexi was supposed to rest until Aiden came to drive her home, Lexi crawled out of bed, pulling the bag the nurse had brought with her. The bloody contents of the package might be a gruesome souvenir to most patients, but she intended to register it at the lab and study every inch of it to see if there was any trace from her attacker left behind. Although her desperate need for answers wanted her to open the bag and start working, she knew how important it was to preserve whatever was there until she was in the pristine environment of the lab. She had the potential evidence in her custody, and right now, that was all that mattered.

Instead, she opened the bag with her personal belongings, knowing she'd have to dress before she could leave. She held her boots up to the light above the head of the bed, checking the soles for any unusual trace. But if tripping her attacker had pulled anything uniquely identifiable off him, the evidence had gone the way of the missing bootie.

Although her stitches tugged at her scalp when she squinted to study her clothing more carefully, and her head throbbed with every footfall, she was intent on locating anything that might prove useful to identifying her attacker and Jennifer

Li's killer. Once she was convinced there was nothing she could log as evidence, she pulled her jeans on under the hospital gown she wore. Before she put her sweater and blouse on, she spread them out across the bed to study them. Neither one looked very warm and comforting right now. Blood stained the cuffs and collar of her blouse, and her sweater had been cut off her in the ER, so the staff didn't have to pull it over her head. She moved on to Aiden's jacket and cap from the plastic bag with her belongings and added them to the top of the bed.

Her wounds had been treated. Insurance had been filed. She had a printout of concussion protocols with accepted treatments and warning signs that merited contacting a physician again. She'd been checked from stem to stern, with the resulting report that her only injuries were the blows to her head and some bruising on her body. But if Nurse Polly thought she was going to "take it easy" without having any answers, then they didn't know her very well. The attack on Lexi had jeopardized solving Jennifer Li's murder, and it might even have compromised KCPD's investigation into a potential serial killer, if it turned out Jennifer Li's death and Giselle Byrd's murder she'd investigated earlier that week were related.

Sitting still and doing nothing had never been her best thing. And when doing nothing might impact the investigation her team and Detectives

Watson and Kramer were working on tonight, doing nothing would be impossible. Since the doctor hadn't given her a sedative, and recommended over-the-counter pain meds, she wasn't about to fall asleep with her mind racing with the need to work.

She should have brought her kit with her to the hospital and gathered samples as the ER doctor and trauma staff worked on her. She felt like an amateur looking for evidence this way, but at least she was doing something useful. Still, the nurse had purposefully dimmed the lights in the room so as not to aggravate her concussion. And Lexi needed more light if she was going to focus her one good eye and the slit of vision she had in her left eye on anything useful. So she pushed the switch twice, taking the level of light over the bed from naptime in the shadows to piercing Lexi's brain like a fiery hot poker. With three more quick taps, she adjusted the light to its middle level and leaned over the bed, ignoring the throbbing in her skull as she studied the blouse and sweater piece by piece.

Nothing. Nothing. And more nothing.

She needed an ultraviolet light to look for any transfer that was invisible to the naked eye. Lexi shivered in her hospital gown, not feeling terribly inclined to put her stained clothes back on. Instead, she folded them neatly and told herself she would look more closely at them once she had her kit.

When she got to Aiden's coat, she gathered it into her arms and dipped her nose to the collar. She breathed in the spicy, musky scent that was uniquely his and felt a sense of calm seep through her as she exhaled, taking the edge off her frantic need to find answers. Beyond the security of her parents, and Levi's overprotective nature where she was concerned, Lexi had never felt the kind of security she experienced when Aiden was with her. Bully eliminator in middle school. Flat-tire fixer in high school. Shoulder to cry on when her choice in men blew up in her face. He could make her laugh, he could drive her crazy, but she always felt safe with him. She felt as valued and cared for with Aiden as she did her own brother. Maybe because of their opposite personalities, Aiden seemed to bring balance to her world. If her family had grounded him, he had pushed her out of her comfort zone. Get another specialized degree. Take the promotion. Rappel down that cliff. Dump the guy who made her cry. He was that bolster of support who assured her of her strength, that devil's advocate who helped her clear her thoughts so that she could make informed decisions. He was that solid foundation that gave her the confidence to do and be everything she wanted to be.

But something with Aiden had felt different tonight. The way he and Blue had charged into that hotel room to find her. The way he'd scooped her up in his arms and wrapped his jacket and body around hers to give her the heat and strength she'd lost. The balance between them had felt off-kilter. She knew him well enough to know Aiden had been afraid for her, afraid she was more seriously injured, afraid she might die. But where did that fear come from? Reliving his own childhood trauma? Worry about failing his promise to Levi? Failing her? Was it possible his feelings were something other than friendship?

When he'd been eighteen, and she'd been a lowly freshman in high school, she'd had all kinds of innocent fantasies about Aiden charging to her rescue like he had tonight. There'd be a kiss, and they'd ride off into the sunset in his truck. The teasing conversations they shared would turn to more serious, more heartfelt topics. She'd have even given him her virginity if he'd asked for it—not that Levi would have been thrilled with Aiden taking advantage of her innocent desires, and not that Aiden would have taken advantage of anyone—and she'd be a willing participant. But since none of that had happened, those fantasies had eventually become nothing more than girlish entries in her journal. Her lusty admiration for all things Aiden Murphy had eventually receded as she matured, and her teenage feelings had gone the way of her journal—packed up in a box and stowed away in a dusty corner of the attic.

If she ever put a name to the grown-up version of that teenage crush that crept into her thoughts on nights like this, it would feel like too much, like she'd be risking all that was good and loyal and comforting between them for something that might not be reciprocated in the same way. Something that wouldn't last. Something that would drive a wedge into his friendship with Levi and destroy the precious perfection of the relationship she shared with him now.

He'd be without a family. And she'd be without Aiden.

Maybe she'd misread the vibe Aiden was giving off tonight. Clearly, she hadn't understood Kevin's feelings for her. She hadn't even suspected he wasn't as committed to keeping their relationship going as she'd been. Not until she'd found him in bed with his executive assistant did she realize just how broken their relationship had become. Apparently, Lexi needed obvious clues she could process, whether it was a crime scene or a relationship. And since Aiden had never once presented any facts for her to evaluate—not one kiss on the lips, no seductive words or love notes, not even an invitation for a date—she couldn't trust her gut that he would ever be interested in something more.

Without any evidence to pursue that line of

thinking, Lexi breathed in the scent and warmth that Aiden's jacket represented one more time before shaking it loose and flipping it around her shoulders to slide on like a familiar hug. But when she pulled out the knit cap that had been tucked inside the sleeve, she paused.

Something thin, light-colored, almost translucent, was caught in the nubby weave.

She moved closer to the light over the bed to study it more carefully. Although, *study* was a relative term. "What I wouldn't give for two good eyes and a flashlight right now."

She remembered protesting when Aiden had pulled off his cap and tugged it down over her hair to anchor a rudimentary bandage and keep her from going into shock. But maybe she should be thanking him for preserving this tiny piece of evidence.

Was it a strand of pale hair? Some other fiber that was too fine to study with the naked eye? It was too light-colored to match Aiden's blue-black hair. It was too straight to be one of her own waves. Too long to belong to Blue. While she couldn't rule out that it was a hair or fiber from Aiden's most recent date, she knew that he didn't wear his uniform when he went out. And he hadn't mentioned that he'd been seeing anyone recently, anyway. Was this tiny anomaly in Aiden's cap something she'd picked up in Jennifer Li's hotel room?

Could it be trace from the man who'd attacked her?

Lexi's pulse revved with anticipation. Maybe her contributions tonight wouldn't be a total loss. She could analyze it later in the lab, as long as she preserved the chain of evidence, and find an answer to who had attacked her or where he'd been or something he'd encountered before coming after her. Anything besides this helpless feeling of not knowing who had hurt her and ended another woman's life tonight.

She surveyed the room for something sterile she could use to preserve the evidence. Her gaze landed on the water cup sealed in clear plastic on the rolling tray beside the bed. She peeled the bag open, then used it to pluck the hair or fiber from the knit cap. She dropped it into the cup and folded the bag shut around the cup. Another quick search led her to the marker on the dry-erase board beside the door. She wrote the time and date on the bag, listed the location where she'd found it, and was adding her initials to the bag when the door swung open.

"Lexi?"

She backed away, barely escaping being hit by the door as a tall blond man strode in. He wore a black tuxedo, wool coat and white cashmere scarf with long fringe. She knew she was in trouble before Kevin Nelson swallowed her up in a tight hug that lifted her onto her toes. "Kev?"

"Oh, my God, Lexi." Her ex-boyfriend and would-have-been fiancé set her back on her feet, rubbing his hands up and down her arms as he leaned back to see her injuries. "Look at you. I came as soon as we could get away from Mother and Father's dinner party. What happened?"

"We?" Lexi palmed the middle of his chest and pushed him back a step, all the while clutching her cup-size bag of evidence in a fist to her own chest. "Kevin, what are you doing here?"

With some breathing room between them, she could look beyond him to see the woman waiting in the doorway behind him. Not the office assistant she'd found Kevin with when they broke up. No, this one was a stunning platinum blonde who wore her silvery evening gown, and what Lexi hoped was a fake fur coat, with the elegant confidence of a woman who belonged in Kevin's privileged world.

"Um…?" Why did she suddenly feel like she'd been hit in the head again? She didn't understand what was happening. "Who…?" She tilted her face up to Kevin's. "Why are you here?"

Kevin stepped to one side to make introductions. "Alexis Callahan. This is Cynthia Sterling."

"His fiancée," Cynthia clarified. She pulled her left hand from the pocket of her ermine-like coat and propped it on her hip in a not-so-subtle show of the diamond cluster on her ring finger.

"Oh." When she felt the weight of Kevin's hand

settling at the small of her back, Lexi moved away, pulling Aiden's jacket together at her neck and hugging it around her body. It wasn't fur and it wasn't fake, but she'd take his KCPD jacket any day over Cynthia's showy outfit. "Congratulations."

Instead of helping her make sense of his presence here, Kevin pulled his scarf from his coat and looped it around his fiancée's neck, pulling her toward him in what Lexi supposed was some cutesy form of intimacy. Though after what she'd seen tonight in Jennifer Li's suite at the Regal Hotel, Lexi found the gesture anything but cute. "Cynthia, would you find us some hot coffee? And maybe you'd better have a seat in the waiting room. I'm not certain yet what Lexi needs from me, and I'm sure there's a rule about having too many visitors and upsetting the patient."

"What I need from you?" Lexi echoed. Cynthia looked about as thrilled to be here as Lexi was to have the company.

"Yes. The hospital called me," Kevin finally explained. "I'm still listed as your emergency contact."

"You are?" He'd left his parents' swanky Thanksgiving soirée to come see an old girlfriend because the hospital had gotten his name from her purse? "I forgot to change it. I guess I haven't needed anyone since we broke up."

The double entendre of her words seemed to go right over his head. "Well, you need someone tonight. I'm glad University Hospital called. You and I have too much history for me to leave you alone at a time like this."

Cynthia's sigh echoed throughout the room. *She* understood Lexi's double meaning. She straightened on her spiky silver heels, and Lexi idly wondered how she'd gotten through the snow in those delicate shoes. "Do what you have to, darling. It's good that you can make the time to help those in need." Lexi wanted to arch an eyebrow at what felt like an insult. Cynthia didn't need to be slinging barbs. She had no interest in staking a claim on the other woman's fiancé. The platinum blonde rested her hand on Kevin's chest a moment before tying the scarf loosely around her neck. "I love that about you. I'll get your coffee and meet you in the waiting area."

"Thank you, darling."

"Nice to meet you, Alexis." Kevin's parents probably loved Cynthia's veneer of impeccable politeness. "I'm sorry it wasn't under better circumstances."

Cynthia's insecurity over Kevin's wandering eyes might be laughable if Lexi didn't know she was smart to be cautious.

But the blonde had nothing to worry about from Lexi. As far as she was concerned, this visit was a paperwork snafu, not a second-chance romance about to happen. She nudged Kevin toward the door. "Go with her. Truly, they're not even keeping me overnight. I'll straighten things out with the hospital."

Kevin planted his feet and faced her. He cupped her elbows and ran his hands up and down her arms. "I want to be here if you need me. I hate that you're alone. I know I screwed things up between us, but that doesn't mean I stopped caring."

"Despite what your fiancée says, I'm hardly a charity case, Kev. And I'm not alone." Although, the emptiness of the room belied that statement.

She had Aiden and Blue. And her friends at the lab. Didn't she?

"Isn't Levi deployed?"

"Yes. But I have other people in my life. I appreciate your concern, but I don't need you." She shrugged off his touch and retreated until her hips hit the bed. "I apologize for the inconvenience, but you should leave."

She wasn't surprised that Kevin followed her into the room to argue his case to square things between them after their messy split or whatever this visit was about. But curiosity pushed aside her annoyance when her gaze zeroed in on a dusting of fibers that clung to the lapel of his black wool dress coat.

Long. Straight. Pale in color and nearly translucent.

Her fingers teased the makeshift evidence bag she'd tucked into her pocket. Unless she compared them under a microscope with a bright light, she couldn't be certain they were a match. But to her bruised, weary eyes in the room's relatively dim light, they looked similar.

Were they fibers from his scarf? Strands of Cynthia's hair? Kevin's hair was combed back and gelled into place. Just how long was his hair?

And was this where her battered brain was taking her? That her ex was a serial killer? Sad to say, but she didn't think Kevin possessed the organizational skills necessary to plot out anyone's demise. But losing his temper? A crime of passion? She remembered him chasing her out into the hallway of their apartment building the afternoon she'd come home early from classes and found him cheating on her. Wearing nothing but a sheet wrapped around his waist, he'd pinned her to the wall and pleaded his case as though it was her fault he'd been naked with his assistant.

What were the odds that she would be the CSI who showed up at the aftermath of his crime? She had a feeling Cynthia would be more cutthroat about killing the other woman. But again, what were the odds that Kevin knew Jennifer Li? His initials hadn't been on those Christmas gift tags.

Unless the attack on her was a separate incident from Jennifer Li's murder?

But why? Kevin had just said he cared about her. In the years they'd been together, her heart and ability to trust might have taken a beating, but Kev had never used his fists. Unless leaving him had brought out a different side to his behavior?

Lexi squeezed her eyes shut. Her mind was racing. Spinning. Her brain was legitimately dizzy and full of far too much wild speculation. She'd conjured up too many possibilities and no concrete answers. She wasn't the detective. She needed those facts, lab analyses, detailed reports to sort out all that had happened tonight.

But with a compromised crime scene, were trustworthy answers even possible?

She was so focused on plucking one of the strands from Kevin's coat that she missed him reaching out to pinch her chin between his thumb and index finger and tilt her face up to his. "Letting you go without a fight was a mistake. Cynthia is everything I thought I wanted in a wife, but there's no fire. I don't love her the way I loved you."

"Ouch!" Lexi slapped his hand away, suddenly wishing she wasn't so good at being independent. What if Kevin meant her harm? And now she was alone with him? "I hope that's not true. If you're going to marry her, you need to love her better than you ever loved me." She slid to one side.

But Kevin followed, keeping her trapped against the bed. "That's not fair, Lexi. We had a lot of good times together. We were a good match. My parents would have come around to the idea of us as a couple, even if you didn't join the company."

"I wasn't involved with them."

"I made one mistake. You're going to throw away everything we could have been because—?"

"Yes!" She shoved at his chest, hating that he was here tonight. "It wasn't right between us, and I doubt it was one time. You didn't want to support me, and I didn't have the energy to support you the way you wanted. It was never going to be."

"Don't say that. We're in a different place now. I'm more mature." Although he gave her the space she demanded, he still reached for her. "I believe coming together like this tonight is kismet, sending me a clear message—"

"Your kismet wouldn't have happened if I hadn't gotten the crap beat out of me tonight."

Yeah, she was betting perfectly posh Cynthia had never uttered a sentence like that.

"But you'll heal. It looks harsh now, but the scarring won't be permanent. You'll be pretty again soon enough. I knew your public service job would eventually come to something like this."

Wow. She really had dodged a bullet by dumping this guy. "Your empathy knows no limit, does it."

"Why are we arguing? I'm here to take care of you."

"It's not your job anymore." Lexi batted his hands away. "You weren't particularly good at it, anyway. I refuse to have this conversation again. If you truly want to help, then leave. I'll change my emergency contact information, so you're not called again."

"I don't mind—"

"That's it, pal. You're done here." A large black gym bag sailed past Kevin's shoulder and landed with a thump on the bed. Aiden followed in its wake, moving in beside Lexi and loosely draping his arm around her shoulders to pull her to his side. His uniform smelled like cold, fresh air, his skin like warm spice. It felt like heaven to have his familiar strength beside her again. "The lady says go, so you're going."

Kevin seemed shocked by the intrusion. "Excuse me, Officer. This is personal."

"Damn right it is. Lex asked you to leave. I'll make sure that happens."

"I'm a close friend of Ms. Callahan's—"

"No, you're not." Lexi curled her fingers into the taut stretch of material between Aiden's flak vest and utility belt. Now she was thanking her good fortune that she'd caught Kev in flagrante delicto and had ended their relationship. "We stopped being close a long time ago."

"Whose fault is that? I won't come groveling to you again." Lexi heard the bite in Kevin's accusation. Aiden heard it, too.

He dropped his arm from her shoulders and took a step toward Kevin. "Nobody asked you to."

"So you've staked your claim on her."

"Staked my claim? She's a grown woman who makes her own choices. And she's not choosing you. Now beat it, before I have to pull out my badge and do something official to keep you from harassing her."

"Aiden." Lexi latched on to the back of Aiden's belt. Kevin was a couple of inches taller than Aiden, and the padded shoulders of his coat made him appear broader, but Lexi knew which man she'd put her money on in a fight. Not that she was going to let the two men get into any kind of brawl in her hospital room. "Take a breath. Please?"

Thankfully, Aiden listened to her in a way Kevin rarely had. She could still feel the wary tension in the muscles of his back, but he turned his stubbled chin to his shoulder to address her, all without taking his eyes off Kevin. "I stopped by the house on the way here. Thought you might want some fresh clothes. Not sure I got all the right stuff, but it'll get you home."

"Thank you. I don't particularly want to put on bloodstained clothes again."

"You have a key to her house?" Kevin raked his fingers through his hair, shaking his head as though the intimacy implied by this man knowing his way around her things confused him.

Oh, if she could only capture one of those hairs as it drifted down onto his coat. But no, she just wanted him gone.

Then Kevin snapped his fingers. "You're Lexi's brother, aren't you?"

Kevin's smile of relief, dismissing Aiden's close relationship as familial, and therefore something he could ignore, grated on what was left of Lexi's raw nerves. She linked her arm through Aiden's, laced her fingers with his and moved up beside him. "My parents fostered him. But we're not related by blood. He's a better man than you'll ever know how to be, and I trust him more than I ever trusted you."

"So it's kinky like that, huh?"

Aiden's grip tightened around hers, and Lexi realized *she* was the one who was losing her temper.

Another man cleared his throat behind Kevin. As Kevin turned, she saw Mac Taylor and his wife, Jules, in the doorway. "Sounds a little heated for a hospital room," Mac observed, taking in Lexi and her visitors.

Julia Dalton-Taylor was a curvy woman with

short blond hair and soft hazel eyes. "How are you feeling?" she asked.

"I'm fine," Lexi assured her.

"You don't look fine." Mac's raspy-voiced observation made her wonder if he was here as her boss or her friend. "Ethan reported what happened. Thought I'd better check in with you."

"I'm sorry, Mac." The confrontation with her ex was temporarily forgotten as she hastened to apologize for failing so miserably her first day heading up her own squad. "I don't know where the guy who attacked me came from. The detectives had cleared the floor. He should have been locked out."

Aiden added his own apology. "If only I'd gotten there a few minutes sooner—this wouldn't have happened, and we'd have the guy in custody. Blue always finds his man."

Mac adjusted his glasses. "Neither of you needs to apologize. I'm just glad you're alive to tell me about it." He turned his sighted eye from Lexi to Aiden. "I appreciate you being there for her."

"Yes, sir."

"Do you mind if I have a look?" Julia linked her arm with Lexi's and pulled her aside to read her chart at the foot of the bed. She pressed her fingers to Lexi's wrist and studied her watch while Lexi kept glancing back at the standoff between Aiden and Kevin. The three men were making introductions, recalling that Kevin had attended a couple of lab staff gatherings with Lexi, but the conversation was more polite than friendly. "Your blood pressure is a little elevated," Jules reported.

"I'm a little stressed," Lexi confessed.

Jules made a notation on the electronic chart. "Ross Muhlbach is a fabulous doctor. Polly Cooper is new, but I've been impressed with her nursing work thus far. You're in good hands."

"I'm not stressed about the care I received."

The older woman's soft smile was all soothing caregiver for a moment before it flatlined. "Mac?"

"What do you need, hon?" The conversation instantly fell silent as Mac excused himself and draped his arm around his wife's shoulders. Jules glanced toward Kevin and Aiden before stretching up on tiptoe to whisper into Mac's ear. "I'm on it." They squeezed each other's hand before he completely pulled away to face the younger men. "Mr. Nelson? You might remember my wife, Julia Dalton-Taylor. She's the senior trauma nurse on staff here, and the director of emergency nursing education here at the university."

Kevin's light blond eyebrows knit together with a frown at the extensive introduction. Still, he offered Mac's wife a polite nod. "Mrs. Taylor."

Mac opened the door and gestured toward the waiting area. "I need you to step outside with me. Ms. Callahan requires her privacy."

Jules pulled the blood pressure cuff from the cart near the head of the bed. "Sooner rather than later would be nice."

Was something wrong with her BP? Lexi sank onto the edge of the bed at the off-duty nurse's direction. But her gaze crossed the room to meet Aiden's blue eyes. They narrowed in concern. "Ma'am? Is she okay?"

The loud rasp of Julia ripping the Velcro apart on the BP cuff sounded ominous. "Officer Murphy, come sit beside the patient. Keep her calm for me."

"Yes, ma'am."

Lexi's fingers felt cold inside Aiden's warm grip. She toppled against his shoulder as the bed took his weight beside her. She didn't try to move away.

Mac pointed to the hallway beyond the door. "Mr. Nelson?"

Kevin reached the doorway before he turned and planted his feet. "Wait. *He* gets to stay? I know you're her brother's sidekick, but—"

"I *want* him to stay," Lexi insisted. Especially if there was something more seriously wrong with her, Aiden was the one she wanted beside her.

Julia Dalton-Taylor proceeded to put the stethoscope around her neck and push the sleeve of Aiden's jacket up Lexi's arm. "Kevin, is it? The patient has asked you to leave. Dr. Muhlbach's orders say Ms. Callahan needs to have a quiet evening. You're not helping."

Mac had no qualms about stepping into Kevin's space and backing him into the doorway. "That lady outranks all of us here. I suggest you do what she says."

Kevin glanced down at Mac, evaluating the subtle threat in the older man's tone. Then, like the man-size spoiled brat he was being tonight, he pointed to Lexi. "*She's* the one who called me."

"The hospital called you," Lexi reminded him. Releasing Aiden's fingers, moving past the nurse tending to her, she grabbed her purse, dug out her wallet and pulled out the old emergency contact card. Then she tore the card into pieces and stuffed it into Kevin's hand. "It won't happen again."

"Shall we?" Mac's terse invitation wasn't really a request.

Kevin was smart enough to finally realize he had no power in this room. He tossed the shreds of paper onto the floor and backed into the hallway ahead of Mac. She wondered if he knew Cynthia was standing right there, holding two cups of coffee, glaring as she listened to every word he'd no doubt have to make excuses for later. "I still care, Lexi. I thought you'd reached out to me. That you'd forgiven me. You gave me hope that we could be a team again. Were you lying—?"

Aiden happily shut the door to block out the useless protests. Lexi picked up the shredded card and tossed it into the trash before sitting on the bed again. "Clearly, I need to update that."

As she pushed her sleeve back up her arm, she realized Mac's wife was packing away the blood pressure equipment and stethoscope. "You two enjoy your evening. I need to go rescue my husband."

"But I thought…"

Jules reached over to squeeze Lexi's knee. "There's nothing wrong with your blood pressure. It was slightly elevated, but not enough to be alarmed. Considering the trauma you suffered tonight and arguing with your unwanted guest, I wouldn't have been surprised if it was even higher." She tucked the equipment back into the cubby beside the bed. "Now, take a couple of deep breaths, let your friend here take care of you a little bit, and congratulations on that promotion."

Lexi imagined she was frowning, although her face was bruised and swollen enough that she couldn't feel much. "Mac's probably reconsidering choosing me after tonight."

"He has no regrets whatsoever. He was only worried about you getting hurt."

"I'll be okay."

"Yes, you will." The older woman extended her hand to Lexi. Although Mac's wife would never be considered a striking beauty, when her lips curved with that gentle, knowing smile, her beauty and compassion shone through, making it easy to see why her boss was so completely devoted to this woman. "I'll leave you two alone."

Aiden shook hands with her, too, before opening the door for her. "Thank you, Mrs. Taylor."

"Good night."

Aiden closed the door behind her. "That is one clever lady. She defused the tension in the room without ever raising her voice. Thinks on her feet." He faced Lexi again. "Like somebody else I know."

"I don't know how that visit got so out of hand. It was just a fluke that Kevin was here. Right?" She unzipped the gym bag Aiden had brought. Her heart warmed at the odd assortment of clothing and supplies he'd stuffed inside—everything from a pair of running shoes and her fuzzy blue slippers, to an embarrassingly skimpy bra she'd gotten as a joke on a girls' night out and only wore on laundry day, thick hiking socks, her travel toiletry bag, a brush and comb, and a chocolate bar. Lexi avoided the bra that made her blush when she thought of Aiden going through her lingerie drawer, and she pulled out the faded T-shirt and Kansas City Chiefs hoodie he'd packed for her. "Don't you take anything he said to heart. There's nothing kinky about our relationship," she asserted, ignoring the whole flush of heat she'd felt at imagining him touching her intimate apparel. "You and I are not related. If he's jealous because I turned to you instead of him, that's his problem."

Aiden raised his hands in surrender to her argument, without confirming or denying whether Kevin's insinuations had gotten under his skin the way they had hers. "My opinion of Mr. Revolving Zipper Pants notwithstanding, I am here for you. You can turn to me for anything. Crowd control. Chauffeur service. Body heat. Whatever you need."

Body heat? She must have heard wrong. Or read a double entendre where none was intended. Those dusty old fantasies locked away in her high school diary kept trying to resurrect themselves. Lexi blamed her aching head for not having better control of her hormones tonight. "I could use a couple of ibuprofen and a ride home."

"Done. I'll catch Mrs. Taylor and tell her your headache isn't going away. Then I'll pull my truck around front while you get changed." He paused with his hand on the door. "By the way, I've got your CSI kit locked up in my truck with Blue. Duvall says it looks like everything inside is accounted for."

Lexi's mood lifted. "That's better news than if you'd brought me a dozen roses and a get-well card. Thank you."

"I know you're not the roses type." He winked and opened the door.

But her happy relief was short-lived as fatigue, self-doubts and fear rushed in. "Aiden?"

Always attuned to her, he heard even that soft whisper. He pushed the door shut and came back to her. "Do I need to call the nurse?" When she couldn't immediately give voice to the thoughts that were bothering her, he touched his fingers to the lock of hair curving over her cheek and smoothed it behind her ear. "Lex? Hey. You know you can tell me anything."

She needed to touch him. She needed a connection, the secure foundation he'd always given her. Lexi reached up and straightened the collar of his uniform shirt and the turtleneck beneath it. Her fingertips might have grazed the ticklish stubble of his dark beard, might have lingered against his warm skin. Her gaze might have zeroed in on the angular line of his jaw and the firm, slightly crooked tilt of his mouth.

His hands slipped beneath the jacket that was long on her and curled around her waist. She was vividly aware of the imprint of ten fingers against her jeans and the bare skin above her waistband. "Hell. You're not wearing anything underneath."

"Too much blood" was all she answered.

And when he would have pulled away, she dropped her hands to grab his wrists to maintain the connection. "No. Don't let go."

His chest expanded with a deep breath he held for several seconds before it seemed as if something inside him let go and he exhaled again. His hands slid against her waist once more, the tips of his fingers settling over the flare of her hips. "Not to be thickheaded, but maybe you'd better explain what's going on here."

"I was scared tonight," she confessed, drifting half a step closer. She curled her fingers into his shirt above his vest, wrinkling the material she'd smoothed a few moments earlier. "I'm an independent woman. I am the home front of a military family. I have three college degrees. I know how to be on my own. Tonight felt different. I was all alone, and I didn't think help was coming in time, and everything you and Levi taught me, it didn't do me a bit of good. And now with Kevin? For a minute, I was scared again. Not just annoyed with him. I don't know who hurt me. What if it was him? What man am I supposed to trust now? I don't like it when I can't figure things out. And I don't like to be scared—"

"You trust *me*. Always." He released her to frame her jaw between his hands, turning her face up to his. "Don't feel guilty about being scared. You're human, aren't you? Being scared is what makes you run or fight. What you have to remember is that you survived. That bastard meant you harm. Maybe he meant to kill you like that poor woman. It's damn near impossible to protect yourself against a blitz attack. A slightly built man or a woman or even a softy like Nelson can overpower you if he or she gets in that first punch." He traced his thumb across her bruised cheek and gentled his tone. "But you didn't give up. You fought back. You got the help you needed. I know you're brave and smart and did everything we taught you to defend yourself. And it worked."

Not very well. "He got away. He stole evidence. Probably ruined the investigation. At least, he made it a lot harder to solve."

"But you survived to still be a key part of that investigation. You *survived*. Never discount how much that means." He paused in his vehement defense of her. He searched her face. For what, she couldn't be sure. And then he dipped his head and pressed a kiss to the corner of his mouth. He lingered long enough for her to feel the soft scrape of his stubble against her skin, long enough for every dormant wish to awaken, long enough for the desire to turn his touch into a real kiss to rush to the spot and tremble beneath his lips. Her pulse was pounding in her ears when he pulled away. "I promise you, help will always come when you need it. *I* will be there when you need me."

Her panties got a little damp at that powerfully evocative promise.

But there were no panties involved with Aiden

Murphy. No sexy bras. No bare skin touching. No kissing. There couldn't be. Her willpower was in short supply tonight. If her lip didn't feel the size of a golf ball, she'd be pulling his mouth down to hers and obeying the crazy urge to turn that buss on the corner of her mouth into a real kiss. But Kevin had already filled the room with awkwardness by calling Aiden her brother. She needed to lighten things up so he could go back to being the Aiden who made her feel physically and emotionally safe again. "Just you? What about Blue?"

That lightened the mood a bit. She did her best to smile, and he chuckled. "Yeah. The dog, too. We're a package deal."

He started to pull away, but she stopped him. Lexi rose on tiptoe and hugged her arms around Aiden's neck, sliding her cheek against his. Her breasts flattened against the hard shell of his protective vest. But the nerve endings in her skin danced in awareness of his ticklish beard stubble and the heat of his thighs crowding against hers. She breathed in his masculine scent and reveled in his unyielding strength.

To hell with awkwardness. Had anything ever felt so good as having Aiden wrapping his strong arms around her?

"Hey."

"Would you stay for a few minutes and just hold me?"

His arms tightened, securing her against him. His breath eased out of his chest and she settled even more closely against him. He gently palmed the back of her head and tucked her beneath his chin. "Anytime, Lex. Anytime."

Chapter Six

"You wanted snow for Thanksgiving, Levi? Here's your snow." Lexi left the illumination of her porch light and turned her computer notebook toward the snow-dusted hedge in front of the bay window of her Craftsman cottage. She made a slow sweep with the computer to capture the layers of smooth white snow that covered her front yard like a blanket of cotton beset with sequins that sparkled in the light from the streetlamp. "Is it too dark to see it? Aiden? A little help?"

Aiden dutifully turned his flashlight to the pretty drifts that had gathered around the evergreen bushes. An online video chat at one in the morning wasn't his first choice as to how this night would end. He'd rather Lexi be inside the house, where it was both warmer and more secure than her front yard. And he refused to acknowledge the inner voice that had had a very clear idea about where he wanted the night to end earlier tonight at the hospital. Whether it was his bed or hers, he'd wanted them to stay just as close as they'd been when she'd insisted on him holding her. But getting close like that—staying close—was dangerous territory.

And so he was holding a flashlight and walking a dog and tromping through the snow, pretending that things were normal and this was enough.

He didn't really begrudge her this Thanksgiving video chat with her brother. She needed the boost in spirit by sharing a little time with her only surviving family after everything she'd been through. She was determined to give Levi this taste of home while he was surrounded by sand and heat.

Aiden glanced over her shoulder to ostensibly be part of the online family gathering. "How's that?"

"Looks like you got snow there early this year," Levi commented.

"And a lot of it."

With Aiden holding Blue on his leash in the other hand, the three of them had taken a walk around the block. He had originally intended to do a quick sweep of the neighborhood to ease his own edgy concerns and give Blue a bit of exercise before turning in. But to Blue's delight, Lexi was bundled up and leading the way out the door before he could get his own coat zipped. Despite every argument to the contrary, he hadn't been able to convince her to postpone the call or to make it from inside the house. She'd claimed the cold air felt invigorating so that she wasn't tired, and the darkness of the night didn't aggravate her headache the way the artificial lights inside the house did. He suspected that the perfectionist in her didn't want to let anything like a blown crime scene, the assault on her or harassment by her ex-boyfriend spoil the plans she had made to celebrate the holiday long-distance with Levi via their biweekly video chat.

She puffed out a steamy breath to make a cloud in the air. "Can you see how cold it is? You'll be able to feel it yourself soon enough."

"It gets cold here, too, you know." Levi plucked at the neckline of his khaki sweater beneath his desert fatigues.

She scooped up a handful of snow and let it float through her gloved fingers. "But you don't get this. You're in the desert, not the mountains there."

"Sis, you don't have to indulge me," Levi chided, laughing at her childish enthusiasm. "You look exhausted."

Lexi shook her head at the rugged, familiar face on the computer screen. "Gee, thanks. It *is* one a.m. our time. I've had a long day."

Even though she said she'd taken a nap this afternoon to help her body adjust to working the late shift, Aiden had a feeling she was running on adrenaline. Excitement at seeing her brother, anxiety about the murder investigation, and probably some lingering fear about going to bed and reliving the assault once she succumbed to the vulnerability of sleep must all be fueling her late-night fun and games. He had a feeling she was going to crash hard sooner than she expected.

But Aiden intended to keep an eye on her and be there to back her up when she needed him— whether she'd admit that need or not. She'd practically melted into him during that never-ending hug at the hospital tonight, as if she couldn't stand on her own two feet a moment longer. Another couple of minutes, and he'd have had to step away from her to keep her from realizing how that cheek-to-thigh press of her curves against his hungry body had affected him. Fortunately, she'd gotten whatever she needed from him to find the strength to pull away and send him out to get her ibuprofen and his truck before his desire for Lexi embarrassed them both.

"I'm the one in a war zone. But you look like you've been through hell. You sure you don't need to be in the hospital?" Levi asked, his face set in a worried frown. "Or at least inside the house? Put Aiden on."

"Oh, fine." She sighed dramatically. "Here. Indulge your bro code."

She took Blue's leash and handed Aiden the computer. He sat on the top step of the porch, keeping Lexi in sight as she took Blue around the yard for another chance to do his business.

"Give me the real scoop, Murph." Levi sounded like the sergeant who ran his own unit and was used to getting things done. "Does she need to be in the hospital?"

Aiden shook his head. "Injury-wise, no. Stitches. Concussion. Cuts and bruises that will eventually heal themselves. As long as she takes it easy for a couple of days, the doctor didn't see any reason for her to take up a hospital bed."

"How is playing in the snow taking it easy?"

"Good luck convincing her to take care of herself. She insisted on being awake for your call since it was a holiday." He scrubbed at his jaw that needed a shave, unafraid to show his own fatigue. "She's also determined that you enjoy your break from soldiering. So work with me here, and keep her stress to a minimum?" He scanned the tent wall and tables and electronic equipment behind Levi. "Looks like you're back at HQ. Did you get to have a Thanksgiving?"

"We're talking about unicorns and rainbows so she doesn't think I'm worried about her?" Levi shook his head and played along. "Food is one thing they do pretty well here. The mess served us everything from turkey to prime rib yesterday. Leftovers in about every dish you can imagine for breakfast and lunch today. Nothing as good as Mom's pecan pie, though."

"Nobody could bake like your mom. I swear I gained ten pounds just that first week I lived with you from all the cookies and fresh bread and welcome cake she made."

Levi nodded, but the two of them could only handle so many unicorns and rainbows, even if it was for his sister's sake. "Enough with the trip down memory lane. Get Lexi inside the house."

A ball of snow sailed over the computer screen and splatted across the middle of Aiden's chest. "Hey!"

"You two are not the boss of me. I was enjoying the fresh air." Lexi had been eavesdropping on their conversation, just as Aiden had suspected. She sat on the step beside him, pulling Blue into a sit between her legs so that the three of them were framed in the camera. "Besides, you know with the time difference that one of us has to make the call really early or really late. I have a three-day weekend coming, so I wanted to take the late call so you wouldn't lose any sleep."

"You have a three-day weekend because you got hurt," Levi insisted. "You should be in bed. Healing."

"And you should be home. Not in harm's way."

"This is my job, kiddo."

"And I was doing mine." Aiden glanced over his shoulder, catching a glimpse of the determination stamped on her bruised face. Yes, she was a scientist who had an eye for detail, ran analyses and wrote reports in jargon he didn't always understand. But she was also a member of law enforcement. She might not wear a gun or make arrests, but that didn't mean she wasn't key to solving crimes and keeping their city safe.

He leaned over and pressed a kiss to the bright red Kansas City Chiefs stocking cap she wore. "I'm sorry, Lex."

She looked genuinely puzzled when she looked up at him. "For what?"

"For going Neanderthal on you tonight. You were doing your job. It was more dangerous than I liked. But I needed the reminder that you're trained to do your job just like Levi and I are, and it's wrong to try to wrap you up in a little package and keep you hidden away where you can't do that job, just so you'll never get hurt." He brushed a wheat-colored wave off her cheek and tucked it inside the cuff of her red knit cap. "I have no doubt you're going to get the guy who attacked you."

"Thank you for saying that."

"You never know when I'm going to have an epiphany."

"Did it hurt much?" Lexi laughed with him as they turned the heavy moment into something lighter and more familiar. Then she touched her fingers to her lips and pressed a kiss to the screen as she stood. "You catch up with Aiden for a couple of minutes. I've got one more Thanksgiving treat to share with you before we hang up. Remember what we used to do after we saw the lights on the Plaza?"

After she'd gone into the house with Blue dancing along beside her in anticipation of a treat, Aiden got up, as well. "Now what is she up to?"

"Um, is there something you want to tell me, Murph?" Levi asked.

"About what?"

The weatherworn sergeant audibly groaned. "About you and Lexi."

Like what? Had he revealed something he shouldn't? *I want to do more than kiss your sister's hat? I want to date your sister? I want to sleep with your sister? I'm in love with her?*

None of those answers came out of his mouth. Instead, he opened the storm door and carried Levi's image inside. "Let's just say after tonight, I have a newfound respect for the work she does. She's out on the front lines like you and me."

Levi seemed to recognize his avoidance of the question and let it slide. "Maybe. But she isn't armed and dangerous."

"No. But Blue and I are." Once inside the door, he shucked his coat and gloves and hung them on the hall tree. "Nobody is hurting her again."

They spent a couple of minutes going over the report of tonight's assault, the clue Lexi had found on the cap she'd been wearing that she hoped could be traced back to her attacker, and strategies for beefing up the security around her house, car and work. He and Levi shared a curse at the snafu that had put her ex and his fiancée in her hospital room. They even ran through a list of coworkers Lexi could rely on to go out on a call with if Aiden and Blue couldn't be there, as well as a list of people they wouldn't want her alone in a room with—like the man she replaced, Dennis Hunt. Levi knew that Lexi was one of the women who had filed a complaint against Hunt for using sexist, degrading language and subjecting the women under his former command to other forms of harassment. Aiden assured Levi that the only reason Hunt was still employed at the crime lab was that he had a good lawyer who was ensuring his client received every step in the penalty process he was entitled to—first, removing him from the complainants and then remediating his behavior. But there weren't many ways he could mess up again that even his lawyer could defend.

Aiden carried the computer into the living room and set it on the coffee table to free up his hands. He sat in front of his friend, his elbows braced on his knees, reiterating a solemn promise. "Trust me, if I have doubts about anyone in Lexi's circle, I'll step in and take care of it. I owe this family that much and more."

Levi cooled his jets, no doubt feeling the same

helplessness Aiden had felt when she'd called to say she was in danger. "It's not your fault that someone put his fists on her. It's just—"

"You're thousands of miles away and used to taking care of Baby Sister."

Lexi cleared her throat with a loud bit of drama as she reentered the front room. Blue trotted in ahead of her, carrying a rawhide chew in his mouth, while she carried a tray with three steaming mugs that had mountains of whipped cream squirted on top. "Excuse me? *Baby* Sister is thirty years old, can hear every word you two are saying, and she doesn't appreciate being called that anymore. I don't know that I ever liked it."

Aiden scooted over to make room for her on the couch as she set the tray down within the camera shot. "Well, I didn't think you'd appreciate being called PITA, either."

"Aiden Royal Murphy," she chided, setting aside the mug she was sipping from and picking up another. "Just for that remark, you can't have this hot chocolate." She took a swallow from that mug, too, leaving a mustache of whipped cream on her top lip. Aiden reached for the third mug, but she snatched that away, too, and hastily drank from it. "Not that one, either." She set it back on the tray, oblivious to the dollop of cream on the tip of her nose. "This one is for Levi."

"Cocoa hog," Aiden teased.

She turned to the screen. "I'm re-creating

Thanksgiving night for you. Giving you a jump start on your holiday. Aiden isn't cooperating."

Levi laughed. "Murph, you got it worse than me, bro. You get to deal with her in person."

"I don't mind." Aiden barely heard the teasing. He was transfixed by the whipped cream on her mouth and the gut-punch of desire to kiss it off her. He wanted to kiss her, period. He could be gentle since she was injured. But more than that full-body hug at the hospital, he remembered pressing his lips to the corner of her mouth. Even with that casual touch, her lips had trembled beneath his. A reaction like that to a simple touch was potent stuff for a man who was fighting a losing battle to maintain the kind of relationship she needed from him.

His body humming with anticipation, Aiden picked up one of the holiday napkins she'd set beneath each mug on the tray and reached over to dab at the corner of her mouth he'd kissed earlier. Despite the swelling and bruising, her pretty green eyes were tilted up and locked on to his, silently asking a question he wanted to answer. Or maybe that was just the question he wanted to read there.

Yeah. He remembered what her lips had felt like beneath his. And yeah, he wanted to kiss her again.

He was marginally aware of Levi throwing his

hands up on the computer screen. "Seriously? Do you two really not see—?"

"What's that?" Aiden snapped out of his lusty trance.

"Huh?" Lexi caught sight of herself in the corner image that reflected what Levi could see. "Oh, gosh. Give me that." Her cheeks warmed to a self-conscious pink, and she snatched the paper napkin from Aiden's fingers to hastily wipe away the glob of whipped cream on her nose.

Aiden must have been too distracted to know what Levi was going on about. "Did you two have a fight, and you're pretending everything is all right for my benefit?"

"Fight?" Aiden frowned. "No, we didn't fight."

"He's been pretty bossy tonight," Lexi pointed out, patting Aiden's knee. "But I think his heart is in the right place. He's protective of me. I just argue back when he comes on too strong."

"I have to sometimes to get you to listen. You get stuck in your head and don't seem to notice the rest of the world going on around you."

"I wish I could order you two to make sense," Levi groused. "Why are things so awkward between you tonight?"

"Awkward?" Lexi scooted the tray of hot chocolate off to the side and pulled the computer closer to the edge of the table. "Aiden's a goofball and I keep him in line. Same old, same old."

"She's stubborn."

"So are you."

"Never mind." Levi put his hands together in a T for time-out, stopping the escalating argument. "I'm too far away to fix anything. You're grown-ups. You'll figure it out." Levi checked his watch and nodded to someone behind his computer screen, probably the next Marine waiting for his or her chance to call home for Thanksgiving. "I need to wrap things up," he explained. "Are you certain this assault is a onetime hazard? Is she safe on the job?"

"I've got this under control." Aiden had already chatted with his supervisor in the K-9 unit, Jedediah Burke, about making him and Blue, or another K-9 team, available for every crime lab call until they were certain the lab staff wasn't being targeted. Especially if this strangler struck again, since he'd already proved he wasn't above assaulting an unarmed criminalist to cover up the clues to his crime.

Lexi pushed into the camera shot. "*We've* got this under control. Don't worry about the home front, Levi. You keep yourself safe."

"Keep your head down, buddy. Blue and I will keep an eye on things here."

Levi considered both their assurances, then nodded. "Well, I trust the dog, at least. Good boy, Blue." The dog raised his head at his name and trotted over to nuzzle the screen. They all laughed when he cocked his head in response to

Levi's voice. "You keep an eye on those two, fur face. Give him a tummy rub from me."

Aiden patted Blue's flank while Lexi scratched the dog around the ears. "Will do."

"I love you, sis."

"I love you, big brother. Can't wait till you're home for Christmas."

"Me, either. Murph? You keep her safe."

"Always."

"Kandahar out."

Once the video chat ended, Lexi and Aiden fell into an awkward silence, punctuated only by Blue's panting and a mournful whine that had the desired effect. Lexi patted the sofa, and Blue, needing no more invitation than that, jumped up between them, stretching his legs and body out to fill up all the available space, plus a little more, reminding Aiden of a toddler climbing into bed with his parents.

Now that the camera was off and she wasn't putting a happy holiday spin on everything for her brother's sake, Lexi closed the computer and sank into the back of the couch with a weary sigh. She accepted Blue's paws across her lap and stroked his exposed chest and tummy. "You didn't have to tell Levi everything that happened tonight, did you? I was trying to keep things light and nostalgic. He'll worry."

"He's a big brother. He's going to worry whether you tell him or not." Aiden was concerned about the utter fatigue in her posture and wished she'd let him take care of her the way she insisted on spoiling Blue. "I told him the facts so he wouldn't imagine anything worse."

"I suppose you're right." She waved her hand in front of her face. "It's not like I can hide this from him."

"Think about how you'd feel if you knew Levi had been wounded or his unit ran into an IED and you heard there were casualties." He ran his fingers across Blue's shoulders until he could capture her hand on the dog's chest. "You'd think the worst, wouldn't you? Until you knew the facts and could process them through that beautiful brain of yours?"

"I hate that you're right. That's a scenario I never want to imagine." Lexi turned her hand and laced her fingers together with his. "Not the Thanksgiving I was hoping for."

Aiden shrugged. "Christmas will be better."

That earned him a glimpse of a smile. "I hope so. Sorry about the hot chocolate. I'll make you another mug."

Before she could push herself up, he picked up one of the mugs she'd sipped out of. "I'm not afraid of sharing a few germs. This one will do." He handed another mug to her and raised his in a toast. "To Levi."

She clinked her mug against his. "To Levi."

They shared several sips of the creamy, chocolaty brew before he realized they were both sagging back against the couch pillows, with the length of a sideways Belgian Malinois stretched between them like a furry chaperone. He heard a soft chuckle. "I'm glad he feels at home here. I hope you do, too."

"I spent more time growing up in this place than I did in my own house. I always feel at home."

"Maybe you'd better get going as soon as you finish your cocoa. It's already late."

Aiden shook his head. "Blue and me are sacking out on your couch tonight."

"But—"

"Nonnegotiable, Lex. You need a good night's sleep, and you won't get that trying to watch your back while you mentally relive every moment of what happened tonight. I've got an overnight bag in my truck. We're staying."

"I—"

"I know you." He sat forward to put his mug on the tray. The moment he straightened, Blue popped up into a sit, ready to move with him. "Easy, boy." He smoothed his hand over Blue's head and looked past him to Lexi. "Mac said you weren't supposed to report back to the lab until Monday. But you've got a mystery to solve, and you aren't going to truly rest until you figure out the who and the why and the how. At least, I can relieve you of the burden of worrying if he's coming back and not feeling safe. You use that brain and do the science. Blue and me? We're the muscle. We'll protect."

After a moment of looking between him and the dog and evaluating his argument, she nodded. She pointed her thumb over her shoulder. "There are four bedrooms in this house. You don't have to sleep on the couch."

"My old room?"

"I changed the decor, but yeah. There's still a bed in there for you." She leaned over the dog to squeeze his knee. "Thank you. And FYI, it's not all those muscles that make me feel safe." Every nerve in his body rushed to that simple touch. Something warmed inside him at her cryptic words. Maybe she was talking about trusting him. Or the familiarity of shared history. Maybe she was talking about the gun and badge he wore. Maybe she was talking about Blue. Didn't matter. He made her feel safe. He was getting the job done. He hadn't failed her after all. The reassurance washed over him, taking the edge off his emotions that had been all over the place tonight. Her faith in him was both daunting and soothing, and made his heart swell with the connection they shared. All that because of a simple touch and some soft words. No wonder the dog leaned into her when she hugged the pooch around the neck. They both had a thing for Lexi

Callahan. "Thank you, too, good boy. Does he need a blanket?"

"Nah. He'll probably sleep at the foot of the bed with me. If that's okay?"

"You can sleep anywhere you want, Blue." She kissed the top of the dog's head and pushed to her feet. She picked up the tray of mugs and headed to the kitchen, the fatigue of the day evident in every shuffling step. "I'll put out a bowl of water for the dog."

"Put out two bowls. I always keep a bag of kibble in the truck. I'll feed him after I settle in."

Aiden bundled up and walked Blue one last time, scanning the neighborhood and giving the outside of the house a good look to ensure everything was secure before he grabbed his go bag from his truck and headed back inside.

Lexi's door was already closed by the time Aiden flipped on the light in the bedroom where he'd lived for eight years. The space was more generic now, painted a taupe color with navy blue curtains. But he recognized Lexi's favorite color in the shots of turquoise in the quilt and the knobs on the dresser. It was a lot more sophisticated than the glow-in-the-dark stars on the ceiling and movie posters that had once decorated the walls.

He changed out of his uniform into jeans and a T-shirt, pulled on a pair of cotton socks and secured his gun in the lockbox at the bottom of his bag. Instead of going straight to bed, he and Blue wandered down the hallway as he re-acquainted himself with the house, checking security at each door and window. After his late dinner, Blue padded along with him. Lexi had taken over the master suite her parents had once occupied, turned her old bedroom into a home office and given Levi's a new coat of paint, although the Kansas City Chiefs helmet lamp Levi had gotten for Christmas one year was still on the table beside the bed.

Aiden hadn't been lying when he'd said he felt at home here. A lot had changed since he'd moved out and gotten his own apartment. But those changes were superficial. This Craftsman-style home might have been updated over the past few years, but at its core, it was solidly built. It represented the family who had lived here and taken him in. It was warm, full of color and life. There were homey smells and familiar sounds—the creak of the hardwood floors, and the hiss and pop of the radiators as they heated with steam from the furnace downstairs. He didn't need to turn on the lights to find his way, partly because of the moonlight and illumination from the streetlamp out front reflecting off the snow through the living room's wide bay window, but mostly because he'd walked these paths so many times.

The first twelve years of his life, he didn't know

if he'd have a house or apartment to go home to, much less his own bed to sleep in. If Patrick Murphy had his drinking buddies over, they'd pass out on whatever flat surface was convenient. Each of his stepmothers had tried to create a home. But a drunk Patrick Murphy couldn't keep a job to pay the rent or put food on the table. And when the current wife tried to make changes or couldn't live up to his "sainted Gail's" memory, things got nasty. The cops would come, and the stepmothers would leave. Sometimes, he'd be taken to a shelter, but more often he'd be left alone with the dad who blamed him for his mother's death. His choices had been to endure his father's wrath and wait for him to pass out, or to run away.

He'd survived until Levi had invited him to come home to dinner with him one night.

And then he'd lived. He'd healed. He'd thrived.

A clean house filled with happy sounds. A full belly and kind words, healthy family role models and a safe place to call home had changed him. Saved him.

The refrigerator light was almost piercingly bright in the twilight of the kitchen when he opened it to pull out a bottle of water. But his eyes adjusted quickly after he closed the door and headed out to the front room. He stopped at the mantel to look at familiar pictures and felt lucky to be included in the display of graduation photographs, a shot of Levi earning a commendation at Camp Pendleton and a church directory photo of Lila and Leroy Callahan taken shortly before their deaths.

"Thank you," he whispered, caressing the corner of the picture frame as he almost always did when he came to the house. "I'll do right by your daughter," he promised before turning away and crossing to the bay window.

Blue braced his paws up on the bench seat in front of the window, mimicking Aiden's watchful stare out into the night. A few houses on the block still had lights on and extra vehicles in the driveway, indicating family and friends were still up late celebrating Thanksgiving, or maybe getting an early start gathering for their Black Friday shopping. But other than the streetlamp in front of Lexi's house, her side of the street seemed to be dark, quiet. This weekend all that would change, he guessed, when the neighbors started putting up their Christmas trees and holiday lights. He suspected Lexi had plans to go all out with the festive decor herself since Levi would be here for Christmas. He wondered if she still kept the artificial tree and multiple boxes of lights and ornaments up in the attic— and if she planned on pulling down the attic stairs and going up there herself to carry them all down here.

He'd add that to his to-do list. Watch over Lexi. Do whatever he could to lighten her responsibilities so that she could rest and recover. He wasn't much of a cook without his barbecue grill, but he could do a lot of other stuff for her while he was here at the house. If tonight's video chat with Levi was any indication, he doubted she'd slow down enough to take care of herself. Although he admired her drive and determination, those traits made Lexi her own worst enemy. Maybe that was the best way he could help over the next few weeks. It sounded like an oxymoron, but he could force her to relax a little and let him do more around here. Let her surrender a little of her control and rest up for the next few days— allow the sanctuary of this house to heal her the way it had once healed him.

Aiden swallowed another long drink of water before capping the bottle and heading back to the couch. Blue curled up on the seat beside him as he leaned back into the cushions and stretched out to put his feet up on the coffee table. No shoes, nothing breakable—as long as he set the bottle on a tray or coaster, Mrs. Callahan would have allowed it. He needed some time to let the thoughts racing through his mind settle. For Lexi's sake, and maybe his own well-being, he needed to have a plan in mind on how he was going to move forward—not just taking care of her this weekend, but how he was going to handle the 24/7 watch he intended to keep until her attacker was caught.

How could he have dropped the ball so royally tonight and let Lexi get beaten like that? True, like every other available cop, he'd pulled extra duty tonight, and had to be called off working the Plaza crowd to assist the CSIU at the Regal Hotel. And how the hell was he was going to keep his hands and heart to himself since guard duty required sharing close quarters, driving to and from work together, and shadowing her at crime scenes? At least until Levi came home, and *he* could keep an eye on his headstrong sister.

And once this guy was caught, what was Aiden going to do? How long did he put his life on hold, wanting a woman, waiting for a relationship that probably shouldn't happen? Nope. Not probably. Even though Kevin Nelson was a self-entitled ass, he'd been right about one thing. Lusting after Lexi, falling in love with her, all felt a little kinky. And not in the good way. Was he strong enough to walk away from the best thing that had ever happened to him? Or was he doomed to suffer these confusing, unrequited feelings?

Or, hell, did he take the risk and tell her the truth?

Yo, Lex. I know the world thinks of me as your second big brother, but, um, you are an incredible woman. Pretty. Brave. Funny. Strong. Sexy. Smart. From the time I was twelve years old, you made me feel I was worth something. And I'm in love with you.

Would the truth destroy the bond between them?

Would simply mentioning his feelings suddenly make it all awkward between them?

Were those his choices? Irreparably damage their friendship by betraying his promise to Levi and Leroy and Lila Callahan? Or sacrifice his heart and walk away to preserve his pride and Lexi's trust?

Didn't sound like there was a winning side to that debate.

He heard the soft click of a door opening, and a few seconds later, he heard Lexi's voice at the entrance to the hallway. "Looks like I'm not the only one who can't sleep."

He set down his water bottle and turned to find her leaning against the wall, wrapped up in a teal-and-turquoise afghan over her pajamas. A dozen thoughts crossed Aiden's mind—how adorably rumpled her hair looked after tossing and turning on her pillow, the trip down memory lane to the Christmas when Lila Callahan had crocheted afghans for the three teenagers in her house. His was royal blue and gold and draped over his couch at his apartment, whereas Levi's had been bright red and gold, like his beloved Chiefs football team. Was Lexi cold? Had he worried her with his restless prowling? Did it feel different to have someone else in the house where she lived alone unless Levi was home on leave? Was she worried about him? Thinking about the case? Had a nightmare wakened her? Did she have any clue how much she meant to him?

Every thought whisked by in a matter of seconds, and Aiden reached out, too tired to fight them both at this hour. He scooted Blue off the couch and held out his hand. "Come here."

That she didn't hesitate to join him was both soul-soothing and a torpedo to any chance that he could keep things platonic between them. He draped his arm around her shoulders, and she cuddled close to his side. "Blue's spot is still warm. You're warm." He felt her relax, sinking into him until he could feel the swell of a small, perfect breast caught between them. "I feel like I can breathe again."

Aiden nodded. Holding her like this was pure torture. Perfect contentment.

"What are you doing, sitting out here alone in the dark?" she asked, drawing mindless shapes across the front of his shirt with her fingers. "Penny for your thoughts?"

He stilled her wandering hand against his chest. "I don't think we can afford what I'm thinking."

Her chin stretched with a big yawn. "What does that mean?"

"Go to sleep, Lex."

"I will if you will." She kicked off her fuzzy slippers, curled her legs up beside her and snuggled in. "I like it when you hold me. More than

I should. Doesn't feel kinky." She yawned again. "Feels good."

"Yeah." He couldn't argue the facts. "It does."

"I wish…" She sounded so drowsy, but her fingers had started their curious exploration again.

"Yeah?"

Her hand stopped and splayed over his heart. "Whatever happens…you're not my brother." The tips of her fingers dug into his pectoral muscle, and parts of his tired body perked up at the unintended caress. "A friend, yes, but…" She pulled her hand back to trace the roses inked above his elbow that represented her parents, and the Celtic knot for his Irish heritage, and then followed the winding scroll of the Serenity Prayer that circled his forearm. "Sexy man. Big heart. Loyal to a fault. Good with dogs… Someday I want to find out if you're a lousy kisser."

"Excuse me?"

"I seriously doubt you would be. But it might help."

Help what? Between the yawns and the mumbling, she wasn't making much sense. "Lex, did you take any kind of medication that the doctor gave you?"

She shook her head. "Wrote in my high school diary about you… Lots of kissing… One day…" Maybe she was already falling asleep, and she was babbling whatever dream or odd thought was going through her head.

Still…she wanted him to kiss her?

Not that he understood what the *lousy* part was about, but she'd imagined *lots of kissing*?

Was this what Levi had picked up on from three thousand miles away? Some sort of sexual tension simmering between him and Lex? The gut-deep emotions that had been stripped away by the possibility of losing her tonight? Did Levi suspect he was tired of playing big brother to Lexi? And if Lexi was changing the rules of their relationship, seeking out his embrace, talking about kissing, then he wasn't sure he could maintain the status quo on his own. How was he going to keep his word to Levi and stuff these feelings back into Pandora's box when Lexi was taunting him—perhaps subconsciously—to break those rules? When she was rested and feeling better, she might not even remember the things she'd said to him tonight.

But he couldn't forget them.

One day…

Words of hope? Or an injured, weary mind reliving some teenage fantasy?

A few minutes later, when she was snoring gently against his chest, Aiden stretched out along the sofa, settling Lexi on top of him. Despite the layers of flannel and denim between them, the guilt and confusion inside him eased as her legs tangled with his, linking them in the most intimate of ways. Her tranquil sigh vibrated through him, her soft weight growing slightly heavier as she relaxed. Aiden pulled the afghan over them both. "Blue." He softly called the dog up on the couch to lie beside them and add his warmth and the protection Aiden trusted without question. If he dozed off, Blue would keep watch.

He might not have forever with Lexi in his arms.

But he had tonight.

Chapter Seven

"You really don't understand the concept of a day off, do you." Aiden strode into the living room, carrying the long plastic tub with the family's artificial spruce tree inside. He winked as Lexi looked up from the couch while Chelsea O'Brien read a list of names over the phone at Lexi's ear. "This is the last of them marked *Christmas*. Do you want me to start putting this together? Don't suppose you found the tree skirt yet, did you?"

Lexi briefly took the phone from between her shoulder and ear and pointed to the braided rug in front of the bay window. Then she got up to retrieve the Christmas tree skirt from the tub she'd opened and tossed it to him, hoping he understood he was in charge of assembling the tree while she paced past Blue gnawing on his rawhide treat. While she appreciated Aiden using his muscle and a better sense of balance than she was sporting this weekend to haul the holiday decorations down from the attic, she was anxious about letting so much time pass between her attack and getting to the office tomorrow morning. If she was feeling well enough to put up Christmas decorations, then she was well enough to start gathering information about Giselle Byrd's and Jennifer Li's killer.

Besides, it seemed a lot smarter to focus on her current investigation than on how quickly she'd become accustomed to having Aiden in the house with her. They'd shared meals, watched a couple of their favorite Christmas movies— singing along with one and quoting their favorite lines from the other. He'd doctored her injuries, taken Blue on routine patrols around the house and neighborhood. Despite her wish that he had some bad habits that might make him less attractive, he neatly folded his clothes, and he helped clean up the kitchen after meals.

She was still holding out for him being a lousy kisser. That might be the one thing that could curtail these feelings he resurrected in her.

But then there was the dangerous habit of falling asleep on the couch she'd developed the past few nights. Well, not exactly on the couch. She'd fallen asleep on Aiden. She'd snuggled up to the furnace of his body, feeling sheltered and content, with his hard body to lean against and his arm draped across the back of the couch behind her shoulders. But she'd awakened to find herself shamelessly sprawled across his chest, the tips of her breasts clutched into tight points where they rubbed against him, the crown of her hair tucked perfectly beneath his chin. This morning, her thigh had been wedged between his legs and she'd felt the evidence of his arousal pushing against her hip. They'd been fully clothed—she in her pajamas and Aiden in jeans and a T-shirt. But it hadn't made a bit of difference to her body's hungry female response to the lure of his masculine contours. Before she was fully awake and aware she was doing it, she'd squeezed her legs around his muscular thigh and rolled her hips, subconsciously trying to ease the liquid pressure pooling at the seam of her legs. That was when she felt the warm hand clamp over her bottom to keep her from rubbing herself against the delicious heat.

"Lex." Her name had come out husky and sharp from Aiden's lips, waking her completely from her semiconscious wantonness.

"Oh. Um. Sorry? I... Sorry." Lexi had set a record for scrambling off the couch and hurrying into the bathroom to get into the shower. Even turning the water to a cooler temperature couldn't seem to wash away the heat lingering on her skin. Each drop of water pricked her like a tantalizing caress, reminding every nerve ending how it had responded to the feel of Aiden's body pressed beneath hers.

And when she finally turned off the chilly spray, wrapped herself in a towel and stepped out into the adjoining bedroom, Aiden was standing there in the doorway to the hall, his sexy, stubbled, stupidly caring face lined with concern. "Everything okay? You were in there almost twenty minutes. I'm sorry if I startled you or made you self-conscious. Nothing happened. You weren't doing anything you shouldn't, and I was holding myself still so I wouldn't wake you up. I'm sorry if I embarrassed you. A guy's body does what it wants to, sometimes."

Apparently, a woman's body did, too. "I'm sorry if I embarrassed *you*. These past two nights have been the best sleep I've had in ages. Thank you." She clutched the towel around her breasts and raked her fingers through her wet hair, sprinkling water on her bare shoulders and into the rug beneath her feet. With the swelling in her face having receded, she could feel her cheeks coloring with heat. "What would Levi say if he'd come in and found me basically dry-humping you?"

Those blue eyes bored into hers. "I'd tell him to mind his own business."

"Aiden…" She'd been joking, trying to make light of their unintentionally intimate sleeping arrangements. "I just meant that he'd probably give us both some grief."

"I don't care who he is or what promise I made. He doesn't get to upset you."

Aiden sounded…serious. Protective of her

subliminal desires. As if her need to wrap her body around his hadn't embarrassed him at all. As if he might be a little mad that *she'd* been embarrassed by it. As if he was struggling with whatever was happening between them every bit as much as she was, and he didn't want her to think she was in the fight alone.

He blinked and the possessive timbre of his voice disappeared. "Now get some clothes on, woman. I need to put a fresh bandage on your stitches and then we've got a house to decorate for Christmas."

Why did everything about that man have to be a turn-on for her? From the fascinatingly complex tats on his warm skin to his sexy voice and sense of humor, his protective, caring nature to those wonderfully strong arms that chased away every fear, every stressor, every thought except security and peace when they closed around her.

"Lexi?"

That wasn't Aiden's voice calling to her. It was a woman's voice. On her phone.

Two hours later and she was still replaying that run-in in her bedroom with the towel and the eyes and the... Oh, damn. Not only was she ignoring her phone call with Chelsea, but she was staring at Aiden kneeling on the rug, sorting out the pieces of the tree. She was measuring out the width of his shoulders, the tapering down to his waist, the deliciously firm curve of muscle in the back of his jeans. She was still reliving the feeling of him holding her, the feeling of being sandwiched between his palm and his body's obvious interest in her, the feeling that he would go to bat for her—against an attacker, against her big brother, against her own self-doubts—if that was what it took to protect her.

No wonder she'd sent him up to the attic and had spent most of the morning on the phone with Chelsea. She'd had to dive into work to keep her thoughts off the man she was falling in love with. Not some high school crush. Grown-up love. Real love.

Love that his overdeveloped sense of responsibility would never allow them to share. Love that was way more complicated than simply obeying what the heart wanted.

"Lex?" Aiden talking. Here. Now. He'd turned around and those blue eyes were staring at her, narrowed with concern. "Everything all right?"

Snap out of it!

Blinking away her thoughts and dreams and despair, Lexi turned away and focused on the phone call. She wasn't the only one from the lab working off the clock on a Sunday afternoon. "Sorry, Chelsea. Say that again. Aiden was distracting me."

"I should be so lucky," Chelsea teased, although Lexi doubted her friend understood the depths of her distraction with Aiden Murphy.

"Tell him hi. And give Blue a tummy rub for me." Since the working dog and his handler were inseparable, Chelsea knew that if Aiden was at the house, then Blue would be, too.

"I will. The key card?" she prompted.

"Right." She imagined Chelsea adjusting her glasses on her nose and reading the information off her computer screen. "I've identified the Regal Hotel master key card that was used to access both of the ninth-floor landing doors, the victim's room and Room 921 directly across the hall—all within the time frame when the ME says Jennifer Li was killed. The card was used again on the landing and in the utility closet on the eighth floor and the first-floor stairwell within the hour that you were attacked."

So that was how the perp had eluded the police and their search of the ninth floor. He'd simply hidden out where they weren't looking. And then he'd waltzed out and joined the guests being held in the lobby and restaurant, probably changing his clothes and blending in with the crowd without raising anyone's suspicions before he left the building.

"The card number belongs to one of the assistant managers," Chelsea went on. "I've got his name, but he's not our guy. He broke his foot at work on Wednesday and has been in St. Luke's Hospital since then. Apparently, a cart loaded with supplies overturned on him. It would be a breach of confidentiality with the hotel, but I suppose he could have loaned the card to somebody."

"Or someone stole it." Lexi thought about the chaos that could ensue with a public workplace accident. There'd been enough EMTs, police, guests and hotel staff on the premises when she'd been hurt at the Regal. It'd be easy enough to lose track of a key card. Hell, she'd lost evidence and her hat—a small rectangle of plastic would be easy enough for someone to pick up. She wondered if his accident could have been staged on purpose, just so the perp could get a hold of that master key. "Let's get his name to the detectives so they can ask him about it."

"Will do."

"Can you find out who was staying in Room 921?"

She heard Chelsea's fingers tapping over the keyboard. "Let's see… Paul and Margaret Montgomery."

"Do you have a picture of them?" Could Paul Montgomery be their killer? Or had they been down on the Plaza watching the lighting ceremony while the mystery guest with the key card had sneaked in to wait in their empty room? "What are the camera angles on the ninth floor? Any shots of someone coming and going out of rooms 920 and 921? Or using the master key elsewhere? Did they come into contact with Jennifer Li anywhere else in the hotel?"

"Um…" Why was Chelsea hesitating? "I'd

need a court order to look at their camera system to see who was actually using the key card. I mean, I can hack into it if you want me to, but if you want to use anything I find in court..."

Right. Although the lab could process the video, it needed to be collected through investigative channels to be usable as evidence. "Request the court order."

"Me?"

"I don't want to wait any longer than necessary. If our perp has full access to the hotel, then he could get into the security office and erase any evidence of him moving through the hotel. Maybe he already has. Even then, we could track the missing footage. Firm up our time frame."

"Sure, I could do all that. But you know who approves the paperwork for that now, right?"

"Dennis Hunt." Lexi paused. She hadn't been picking up the tentative cues in Chelsea's voice. She'd lovingly describe the other woman as quirky or eccentric. And though she tended to be shy in social situations, when it came to work, Chelsea was a clever go-getter who loved to be challenged. "Is there something wrong, Chels? I know Dennis is a first-class jackass, but this is just a matter of typing up the form and getting him to sign off on it, so we can take it to a judge."

"What if I type up all the info, and you present it to him?" she countered.

"Chelsea?" Lexi hugged an arm around her

waist, feeling a real concern for her friend's odd behavior. "Did something happen Friday while I was gone?"

"Nope. Not at all." She answered so fast that Lexi suspected it was a lie. And lying was one of the few things Chelsea didn't have a talent for. "I'm sorry. I know I should be braver, but Dennis gives me the creeps."

"What aren't you telling me? Did he say something to you in slimy Dennis-speak?" That question got Aiden's attention. He came over to sit on the arm of the sofa near where Lexi stood to listen in more closely.

"I haven't seen him since Tuesday of this week. And I'd like to keep it that way."

Lexi sought out the questioning look in Aiden's eyes and shrugged. "I know there's more to this story, and you're going to tell me about it when you're ready, okay? You know you can count on me."

Chelsea huffed a short laugh. "I know. When I'm ready."

Now they were really going to have to talk when she got back to the office. "All right. Get the request together, and I'll deal with Dennis."

"Now I feel like I'm letting you down."

"Uh-uh. Don't go there." Lexi paced back and forth, gesturing as though Chelsea could see her in person. "I'm the boss, aren't I? Ultimately, if it needs to get done, it's my responsibility. But

I also intend to protect my team. Send it to my email and I can print it off here. I'll get a hold of Dennis and have Aiden run me in to the lab. And then to whatever judge we can rustle up on Thanksgiving weekend." He met her gaze and gave a reluctant nod. "Will you be there tomorrow morning to work your computer magic?"

"Whenever you need me. I can come in twenty-four seven." Chelsea's sigh of relief was audible. "I'll spell out what we need from the hotel and get that to you ASAP."

"Good woman. And, Chels? Are you sure you're all right?"

"I am now. Thanks for understanding."

Only, Lexi wasn't sure she did understand as they ended the call. She sank onto the couch beside Aiden and opened her laptop to type up notes from the call.

"Is Chelsea okay?" Aiden asked.

"She says yes, but I don't believe her." Lexi tilted her chin to look up at him. "Something's got her spooked. Something to do with Dennis Hunt. I wonder if she's just more sensitive than the rest of us about the things he says and does. She grew up in the foster system. Dennis might not be the first jerk like that she's run across."

"She lives on her own, right?" Aiden pushed to his feet and went back to hooking together the last limbs of the tree.

"Except for the cats. Peanut Butter and Jelly."

"Please don't tell me she's turning into a crazy cat lady."

"More like a penchant for taking in strays. She has a couple of senior poodles she's fostering from the shelter, too."

"Do you think Hunt has threatened her? To get her to drop her harassment complaint?" Aiden slipped the last branch onto the tree. "Would she feel better if Blue and I went and checked out her place? At least she can feel safe at home."

"I'm not sure how well the cats would take to Blue." The dog raised his head at the mention of his name, and Lexi reached down to pet him. The muscles in his shoulders quivered in anticipation at the opportunity to go to work. "But I think *I'd* feel better if we looked in on her."

He surveyed the tubs scattered across the living room and the stacks of ornament boxes she'd unpacked on the coffee table. "You're not putting all this stuff out, are you? We'll be here all day and night."

"No. But I'm not sure what's in each box beyond the tree. I figured I'd take advantage of the time off to consolidate and organize the decorations. Put out Levi's favorite ornaments. Pack the sentimental stuff in its own box. Move stuff I don't use on to the homeless shelter." She glanced up from her laptop. "I should separate the outside lights from the ones that go on the tree, too."

"And when do you intend to sleep?" he asked.

"It sounds like we're going into the office today, too. Meeting Hunt? Calling up judges and stopping by Chelsea's?" Aiden shook his head. "Didn't Dr. Muhlbach and Mac's wife say you were supposed to take it easy?"

"I need to take care of this paperwork to keep the case moving forward."

"And while we're at the lab, you might as well run some tests on that foreign hair or fiber you found on you at the hospital?"

Lexi snapped her fingers. "Good idea."

Grinning, he shook his head. "I'm guessing that was already on your to-do list." He picked up the empty tub and carried it toward the attic stairs. "All right. I can swing by my apartment while we're out and get some extra changes of clothing. We'll finish putting up the decorations tonight."

Lexi saved her work and closed her laptop. "You don't have to drive me everywhere, Aiden. I won't be going anyplace but the lab and a judge's house. Well, Dennis's, if he won't meet me at the office. At some point I need to get my car from work, anyway. You don't have to chauffeur me around."

"Uh-uh." He halted in his tracks and pointed a stern finger at her. "Already had that conversation. I'm with you twenty-four seven until Blue and I have a shift, and then I've made arrangements with Sergeant Burke—" the director of

KCPD's K-9 Corps and Aiden's boss "—to have someone else on the team shadow you if you get called to a crime scene and I can't be there. And while you're at the lab, we'll rely on Captain Stockman and Sergeant King to keep an eye on you."

Lexi wondered if focusing the security details on her would leave other members of her team at risk. But she doubted she'd be able to argue Aiden out of his protective streak until her stitches came out and the bruises faded from her face.

At least he was more than willing to make the trip to Chelsea's small home in the KC suburb of Independence. Her friend greeted them both with hugs and invited Blue up onto the couch for a thorough petting, scattering the cats into hiding. Blue exchanged some sniffs with the senior poodles, but one was blind, and the other stuck right by his side in the bed at Chelsea's feet. They were more curious than concerned about the big, furry visitor.

Blue enjoyed running through the snow in the huge fenced-in yard after he and Aiden checked windows and doors and the separate garage to make sure Chelsea had nothing to worry about security-wise. That gave Lexi a little time alone with Chelsea to share a cup of tea and press her on why her friend's pale skin was shadowed beneath her glasses. Chelsea dismissed it as a lack of sleep rather than explaining anything to Lexi's satisfaction. Not for the first time, she wondered if Robert Buckner, the former KCPD cop turned private investigator, was taking advantage of her kindhearted friend's willingness to help him, making her feel obligated to burn the candle at both ends. Or were her friend's overly cheerful smiles covering up something else? Like the reason she was so reluctant to have anything to do with Dennis Hunt?

Lexi was pleased to see Aiden slip Chelsea his card with his numbers on it as they headed out the door, in case something came up and she needed a cop or a friend...or a visit from Blue. Chelsea had nearly burst into tears at the offer and rose up on tiptoe to hug Aiden tightly around the neck. *"Keep this guy,"* she mouthed to Lexi before catching her in a tight hug, too. "You two are the best. Thanks."

Then they left her there with only her pets and computers and secrets for company. Lexi resigned herself to biding her time until Chelsea chose to confide in her, either as her friend or her subordinate. But when Chelsea was ready, Lexi would do whatever she could to erase that wary fatigue from her friend's eyes.

Once they were at the crime lab with the proper microscopic equipment, Lexi had no problem identifying the fiber that had come off her as a hair. It was impossible to identify the age or even the sex of her attacker simply by looking at the hair. But she was able to extract a tiny bit of connected tissue from the sample where she had pulled it from her attacker's scalp. Although Khari Thomas was the lab's DNA expert, Lexi was able to run a stain chromatin test on the nuclei of the tissue cells to reveal a male-indicative Y body. Confirming that her attacker was a man was no surprise, considering the strength he'd used against her.

It would take another three to five days to put together a DNA profile and possibly longer to run that profile through all of Chelsea's databases to find a match—assuming their killer was in the system. Lexi sent an email to Khari, asking her to work up the results, compare the profile to the potential DNA samples taken from the prostitute's murder scene and any other DNA evidence from Jennifer Li's crime scene, and get back to her as soon as possible. Lexi promised to reassign one of the newly hired chemists to assist her on Monday if she needed help processing the evidence.

While Aiden brewed them something hot to drink in the lounge, Lexi also discovered an unusual substance within the hair follicle. But with only one hair to work with, there wasn't a large enough sample to run both DNA and a substance analysis. She knew the DNA would put her closer to identifying her attacker than learning whatever dye or hair product or even environmental or medical by-product might have been absorbed into the hair.

Besides, Dennis chose that moment to stroll into the lab. He crossed the sterile, brightly lit room, letting out a long whistle as he leaned across the stainless steel table where she was working to study her. "Somebody did a number on you, didn't they? Must have hurt. You sure you should be back to work already?"

"Dennis," she acknowledged without answering the rhetorical question. She suspected the sudden headache coiling between her eyes had less to do with the aftereffects of her concussion and more to do with sharing breathing space with Dennis. "Thank you for coming in."

He pulled off his stocking cap and ran his fingers through his hair, fluffing the short strands to fill in around the marks from his hair plugs. "You're the boss now. I'm the one on probation. You say jump, and I say… Well, you know the rest."

An exasperated sigh buzzed through Lexi's lips as she secured the sample and waited for the printout of her results. "If you're going to keep messing with your hair, I'm going to need you to put on a hairnet. The lab can't afford to have any stray hairs coming off you and getting into our samples."

"You're not wearing a hairnet."

"I'm not flicking my new-grown hair into our

workspace. Surely you haven't forgotten protocols after a couple of days behind a desk?"

Dennis scoffed at the criticism and slipped his hands into his pockets. "I was surprised to get your call. Thought you'd be out of commission longer than you were."

Tucking the printout into the pocket of her lab coat, Lexi headed to the door. "Sorry to disappoint you."

"Oh, I'm not disappointed." He chuckled as he followed her out. "I'm amused. Everyone thinks you're this golden girl who's going to restore balance to the universe. I got results when I was in charge and you know it." Yes, but at too high a cost for staff morale. "Looks like you can't do this job without me." His subtle digs and smug smile reminded her why she and others had filed the harassment complaints.

"I can't do it without your *signature*," she clarified. She waited for him to exit and locked the lab door behind him. "I've got the paperwork for you to approve in my office." She found the words to be a professional, although thanking him for anything felt like she was conceding to the superiority he craved. "Having the court order ready will enable us to hit the ground running tomorrow morning."

Inside her office, she gestured to a chair, which he refused. So she skipped to handing him the court order request for him to read. He picked up a pen, but his hand hovered above the document, hesitating. "Going to intrude on other innocent people's lives the way you've butted into mine?"

"I know it's hard for you to comprehend, but this isn't about you, Dennis. We used to be a team, remember? And our team helped KCPD solve murders." Lexi took off her lab coat and hung it on the outside hook of her closet, her gaze idly skimming over the Advent calendar she'd start opening in a couple of days. She came back to her chair behind the desk but refused to sit and give him any advantage over her. "I know your career has gone sideways, but we still need you to be a part of that team if you can be. Sign off on the court order and help us solve a murder."

"Nice speech. You been practicing that one?"

Lexi was done forcing herself to be nice to the man. "Are you signing the request? Or do I have to go over your head and bother Mac with it?"

"Doesn't this request show bias?" Dennis taunted, unfazed by her threat. He kept right on nitpicking her ability to do her job. "I don't see any court order for video footage from Giselle Byrd's murder scene."

"Gee. I wish I'd thought of that," she responded, letting plenty of sarcasm leak into her voice. "As I recall, you checked it yourself. That hotel didn't have any security cameras outside of the office. Different clientele in No-Man's-Land."

Dennis shrugged, conceding her point. He

scratched his name across the bottom of the document and tossed both it and the pen onto her desk. "Chelsea was afraid to talk to me?" Lexi hadn't mentioned her friend's name at all, but she supposed the requests on the document pointed to their tech expert. For a moment, she considered asking Dennis about the tension between him and Chels. But that felt like betraying a friend's confidence. Dennis tugged on his stocking cap and pulled his gloves from his coat pocket. "But you're not afraid?"

"I'm not afraid to do my job, if that's what you mean. You're a smart man. And you *are* a good criminalist. But your actions undermined the rest of the team."

"Maybe the rest of the team needed to step up their game."

"Maybe you needed to be a better leader."

Dennis threw out his hands in a mock ta-da. "There's the golden girl again, trying to make everything all rosy and right. So I said a few things the wrong way. At least I got the job done. You've been at this, what—four days? You're already pulling overtime to compensate for the mistakes you made at the Regal Hotel."

"Mistakes? I was assaulted."

"And you lost evidence. Do you think that perp would have risked coming back to the crime scene if you were a man?"

"My God, Dennis—what century were you

born in? What woman warped you so badly that you think…?"

There. He was smirking. Laughing. He'd pushed her hot button, and she'd taken the bait and lashed out. She was no better at managing people than he was. Lexi raked her fingers through her hair and let it fall in a messy disarray as she tempered her outburst. "I'm sorry. I shouldn't have said—"

"I always figured when they kicked me upstairs that they'd promote Wynn to take my job. He's been here the longest and has the most experience. He was hungry for it, too. He was ready. Instead, Mac promoted the cheerleader."

"Are you saying Mac should have promoted Ethan because he's a man?"

Chapter Eight

Lexi's mouth opened, ready to argue her qualifications for this job, when she heard the rapid clicking of toenails on the hallway tile. Seconds later, Blue trotted into the office. The dog paused to sniff Dennis's boots before trotting around the desk to Lexi. Dennis watched Blue prop his front paws up on Lexi's desk to sniff at the front pocket of her jeans where she sometimes kept treats. But to anyone who didn't know about the secret stash, it looked like the dog was positioning himself between Lexi and her suddenly unwelcome guest.

She reached out to scrub her hand around Blue's ears, thanking him for distracting her from the rant she'd been about to unleash. It wouldn't have made any difference to Dennis, and probably would have gotten her into trouble. "Who's my favorite boy?"

Dennis grumbled beneath his breath. "Of course, you've got your very own bodyguards. Where's Murphy?"

"Right here." Aiden strode in, carrying two insulated paper cups steaming with the scent of fresh coffee. He walked past Dennis to hand one to Lexi. "I brought the caffeine you ordered."

She gratefully wrapped her fingers around the warm cup and dipped her nose to inhale its reviving aroma. She needed the diversion to keep herself from sinking to Dennis's level. "Thank you."

Aiden propped his hip on the corner of her desk and faced Dennis. Unlike the dog, there was no mistaking that he was purposefully positioning himself between Lexi and her guest. "Didn't know if you'd be staying, Hunt, or I'd have brought you a cup, too."

Dennis's ego kept him from being intimidated. "You don't have to be polite, Murph. I'll have my day in front of the ethics board and prove these accusations have no merit. Then I'll be right back where I'm supposed to be. *This* office." He paused in the doorway and doffed Lexi a mock salute. "Supervisor Callahan."

The moment he was gone, Lexi sank into her chair, closing her eyes and absently resting her hand on Blue's head as exhaustion—both physical and mental—claimed her.

"You sure I can't punch him for being rude, crude and unlikable?" She heard the shift of Aiden's weight off her desk. Her eyes fluttered open when she felt him pluck the insulated paper cup from her hand. He set both coffees on the desk and turned her chair to the side to kneel in front of her. He brushed a couple of loose tendrils of hair away from her bruised eye and bandaged stitches and tucked them behind her ear. He rested his palm at the side of her neck and jaw, his blue eyes studying her face and frowning. "You're pale. Forget the caffeine. I think you've pushed hard enough today."

"It's Dennis who exhausts me. He's right. I blew my first assignment as supervisor."

He stroked his thumb along the line of her jaw in a rough caress. "You didn't blow anything. You were a victim of a crime. No different than Jennifer Li, except you survived. You weren't attacked because you failed. You were attacked because you were doing your damn job, and that was a threat to that creep. Hunt's just trying to get under your skin and make you feel inadequate so he doesn't feel lonely because he's such a loser." His warm, calloused thumb stopped beneath the point of her chin, tilting her face ever so slightly to his. His nostrils flared as he gentled his vehement defense of her from his tone. "Call your judge and let's go home. We'll worry about your car tomorrow."

The warmth of his touch, his caring, his utter faith in her abilities surged through her, giving her a boost of strength. "You always say the right thing to me. Thank you."

She framed his jaw between her hands, leaned

forward and pressed her lips to his. She felt a riot of sensations—the rasp of his stubble beneath her palms, the pinch of her healing lip, the coffee-scented warmth of his startled breath caressing her face in the split second before her lips softened against his. It wasn't a sisterly kiss, but it was chaste, full of gratitude, full of want, full of all the unsatisfied what-ifs she wanted to explore with this man but held in check.

A moment later, Aiden tilted his head slightly, his lips settling between hers like interlocking pieces of a puzzle snapping into place. His response to the contact was equally chaste. But his lips vibrated against hers like the pulse she felt hammering beneath her fingertips at the side of his neck. His breathing grew rapid and gusted against her cheek as he feathered his fingers into her hair and cradled her head to hold her mouth against his for several precious seconds. This kiss wasn't anything like what she wanted to share with Aiden. It wasn't wild or passionate or free-spirited. This kiss was an exercise in self-control, and it felt inordinately hot to sense that any moment now they were both about to fail. They were priming a charge for a detonation. And the payoff would be explosive.

Then his shoulders lifted with a resolute sigh and he pulled away, tugging her bottom lip between his like a tantalizing morsel. It gently snapped back, breaking contact, but arrowing a shaft of heat straight to her womb.

With his fingers still clutched against her scalp, he touched his forehead to hers. Those blue eyes opened right above her, and it was like looking up and losing herself in the fathomless depths of the twilight sky. Oh, man, she had it bad, thinking in metaphors she might have used in the ramblings of her teenage journal.

His eyes, though, were anchored on her mouth. "Your lip is feeling better? It doesn't hurt anymore?"

"Not much."

Was that why he'd held back? Was he afraid of hurting her? He pressed the pad of his thumb to the pout of her bottom lip, and she thought, for just one moment, that he was going to throw that sensual restraint out the window and kiss her.

"Lex…"

Suddenly, a long black snout and lolling pink tongue thrust up between them, forcing them apart. Blue slurped at Aiden's face, stealing the kiss Lexi had wanted.

"And there's the chaperone." When the cold, wet nose turned to Lexi, Aiden pushed the dog down. "Easy, boy." He wrestled the dog onto his back and rubbed his flanks.

Lexi leaned over and added her petting to what was apparently a long-overdue tummy rub. "This explains the sorry state of my love life," she teased. "Too many big brothers. Even the furry one thinks he knows what's best for me."

When she realized she was the only one laughing, Lexi turned her chair away and stood. Maybe she hadn't really meant it as a joke. Aiden wasn't stupid. He had to know how she felt about him—how she suspected he felt about her. But if he was determined to ignore both the chemistry and history they shared, she had to give him his space and let him define the parameters of their relationship. What good was pushing him to share his feelings if he didn't choose to love her? She understood. She'd pined after him for years in one way or another but had chosen not to act on her feelings.

But she could have died the other night. She could have lived her whole life denying herself the chance to love and be loved by Aiden. Lexi wasn't sure how much longer she could pretend the status quo between them was okay, that it wasn't twisting something inside her every day she denied how much she loved this man, how much she needed him to love her.

Aiden nudged Blue to his feet and stood, ordering the dog to follow as he retrieved their coats from the seat of one of her guest chairs. "Let's get you home. I'm not doing a very good job of protecting you if I let you work to the point of exhaustion."

While she slipped on her coat and bundled

up for the cold weather outside, Lexi wondered whether Aiden would have dropped that knight-in-shining-armor vow of celibacy—or whatever was holding him back—if she'd taken the initiative and deepened the kiss herself? She knew he'd been through hell while growing up, with the relationships he was supposed to be able to trust. Being fostered by her family had given him his best friend, wonderful role models and the security every child should be able to enjoy. It probably made sense that he was reluctant to change the status quo and risk losing the only reliable family he'd ever known.

But how could she make him believe that loving her wouldn't be a risk? Was she supposed to be the strong one and force him out of his comfort zone? Or was she being unfair to hope, to insist, that they could be something more?

By the time she had her court order signed by Judge Whitman, and a plan of attack for her team to pursue the investigation tomorrow, the sun had set. Lexi and Aiden had shared a simple meal, then tackled putting up the decorations on the Christmas tree and around the house. She got out all her Mannheim Steamroller CDs and blasted the jazzy Christmas music throughout the house while they worked, curtailing the need for much conversation beyond where to hang this ornament or where she stored the batteries to light up the Victorian holiday village she set up along the bench of the bay window.

By ten o'clock, the lights from the Christmas tree and the Victorian village offered the only illumination in the front room. The hallway light was on behind her because Aiden was up in the attic, stowing the storage tubs. While Blue snoozed on the cushion behind her, Lexi sat on the braided rug between the couch and coffee table, repacking the ornament boxes in the last tub for Aiden to carry upstairs. Cocooned by shadows, the gentle glow of the decorated tree and front window filled the room with a calming sense of peace and enough nostalgia that she felt like she was surrounded by her missing family.

It had been a long weekend, full of physical demands and emotional ups and downs. Lexi was having a hard time keeping her chin up and not dozing off. But she refused to go put on her pajamas, brush her teeth and head to bed, partly because she knew Aiden would insist on finishing whatever work remained to be done himself and partly because she'd quickly gotten into the habit of falling asleep on him. As frustrating as this protective non-relationship with him had become, a foolish part of her desperately hoped that he'd sit down with her for a quiet chat, and offer a sturdy shoulder to lean on and a haven of warmth and strength where she could fall asleep in his arms again.

Her head had tipped back onto the couch and her eyes had drifted shut when Aiden's voice startled her. "Is that last one ready to go up?"

Lexi snapped her head up. "What?"

"Whoa. Sorry." Aiden flipped on the lamp beside the couch and shut off the CD player. "You know, you can shove that beast off the couch and lie down if you're tired." He shooed Blue off the sofa and held out a hand to help Lexi to her feet. "He may be a lean, mean, feisty machine, but he likes you. He'll do what you say."

"I know he will." Lexi sank onto the cushion, stifling a yawn with her hand. But just as quickly, she pushed to her feet. The last thing she needed was to drift off in the place she would forever associate with sleeping with Aiden. Things were already too complicated between them to risk mumbling in her sleep or, worse, discovering she couldn't sleep through the night without his arms around her. Pretending she suddenly had all the energy in the world, she snapped the lid onto the tub. "It's ready to go. I think we've got everything up except for these three sentimental cuties I found."

She picked up one of the three homemade ornaments she'd laid on the coffee table. Two decades old and built out of foam balls, glue, yarn, cloth, pins and children's imaginations, these had been a craft project her mother had come up with one snow day to keep Lexi and the boys busy.

She handed Aiden the one he'd made. Although one of the construction paper eyes was missing, the plastic cup that had been cut to resemble a helmet was still wedged into place on the figure's head. "Mom was pleased with our imaginations. Not one of us made a snowman out of them."

He snickered at his age twelve handiwork. "Nothing says Christmas like an astronaut."

"That's what you wanted to be when you were growing up."

"I think I just wanted to escape. The planet wasn't very kind to me early on." He hung it on a branch, then paused to study the entire tree. "That was the first Christmas I ever had a tree. I remember seeing presents with my name on them underneath, and I didn't think they were real. The first one I opened was a package of socks. But they were new, and they were mine, and lame as they were, I thought it was the coolest thing ever. Your dad got me a bike, and I didn't know how to ride it. Made your mom cry. But he taught me how."

"Which made her cry again." Lexi remembered how quickly Aiden had gone from novice to daredevil, skinning knees and elbows and, ultimately, cutting open his chin, which warranted a trip to the ER. She glanced up, seeing the faint evidence of that scar through the dark stubble of his late-night beard.

"Your parents taught me a lot of things." He tapped the rudimentary astronaut, making it swing back and forth on its branch. "After a while, I realized I didn't want to go anywhere else. I wanted to stay grounded and make this world as safe a place as your mom and dad made it for me."

Tears stung the corners of Lexi's eyes, and she quickly swiped them away. "You'd better take that tub upstairs and close the attic before I haul off and hug you."

But Aiden didn't smile back. He simply nodded, picked up the tub and headed down the hallway.

How did even those teasing threats of affection become so awkward between them? Did he think he was going to lose those memories, that tenuous link to the only family he'd ever known, by developing a more intimate relationship with her? How could she make him see that the bond between them would only grow stronger, deeper? He wouldn't betray her parents or Levi by wanting her. Together, they could expand the family, make new memories, honor her parents by loving each other the same way they had loved.

But that wasn't something she could tell Aiden and make him believe. He'd have to discover the power of that kind of love on his own.

She listened for the creaking of the folding stairs beneath Aiden's feet before turning back to the tree. Bless Levi's heart—he'd always known he'd wanted to go into the military from the time he was a little boy. His ornament was covered in camouflage material and he'd glued the plastic cap from one of his GI action figures on top of its head. Lexi hung his ornament next to Aiden's, then picked up the angel she'd made with its pipe cleaner halo and hung it on a nearby branch.

She needed to focus on work. And healing. She needed to piece together the clues to two murders and her assault. She might be ready to take her relationship with Aiden to the next level, but he wasn't. She needed to respect that and concentrate on the things she could control—like making sure everything at the house was perfect for Levi's arrival on Christmas Eve.

Inhaling a deep breath to clear her head and shut down her heart, Lexi circled around the tree, adjusting the string of lights, moving an ornament to an empty branch, stretching up on tiptoe to nudge the star on top into a straighter position. She was pleased that the tree reflected the colors of the season, and that the whole front room had a special glow that would welcome Santa and remind Levi how much it meant to be home for the holiday.

Lexi was on her knees, smoothing out the wrinkles in the tree skirt, when she caught a blur of movement in the window behind her. What was that? A bird flying through the light from the streetlamp across the street? What kind of bird was out at this time of night on the cusp of winter? Was it some funky sweep of headlights moving the shadows of her porch and the row of evergreen bushes in front of the house?

Feeling a vague sense of unease at not being able to identify the source of the movement, she pushed to her feet and turned to study the night beyond the panes of glass. But before she could discern one shadow from another, Blue barked and charged at the window. "Blue!"

The Malinois jumped onto the bench, knocking her carefully placed houses askew. One teetered over the edge and crashed to the floor.

But it wasn't the shattered decoration that turned her blood to ice. "Aiden!"

It was the hooded figure in black, right outside the window. Faceless black mask. Dark eyes. Black gloves. He gave her a mocking salute before swinging his leg over the porch railing. Snarling a vicious alarm, Blue lunged against the glass and the window bowed. "Blue!"

The figure, startled by the dog's attack, lost his footing and tumbled into the evergreen bushes. He knocked the snow off the bushes as he pushed them aside and scrambled to his feet.

She was suddenly aware of the hard footsteps racing up behind her a split second before strong hands grasped her shoulders. "Lex!" She yelped and turned as Aiden pulled her away from the window. "Blue! Get down! *Hier!*"

He ordered Blue to his side and the dog obeyed, knocking over another ceramic house as he leaped down and dashed to Aiden's side.

Lexi braced her hands on Aiden's chest as he pulled her to the interior wall of the foyer. "Did you see him? Just like at the crime scene. All in black. Watching me. He's running now. Blue scared him off."

"Stay put." Aiden hurried past the coats hanging on the hall tree and pulled his gun.

He unlocked the dead bolt and a blast of cold air swept in as he inched the door open, peering one way, then the other, making sure his path was clear before he gave chase. No! He wasn't facing that intruder alone.

He'd attacked before.

He'd killed before.

Lexi tugged on the sleeve of Aiden's sweater. "Take Blue with you!"

The door slammed shut and Aiden was pushing her back against the wall. His shoulders blocked the world from view, his midnight blue eyes boring into hers. "He stays here. If anyone gets past me, they'll have to deal with him before they get to you."

"If that's the guy, he's not afraid to hurt anyone. He's not afraid to kill—"

Aiden's free hand slipped around the back

of her neck and he brought his mouth down in a hard stamp of a kiss that shocked the argument out of her. Not chaste. Not lousy. Lexi's lips parted and Aiden's tongue claimed what she willingly offered. Her fingers dug into his shoulders, hanging on to every precious millisecond. This kiss was a warning. A promise. An unguarded moment when everything they felt for each other sneaked through.

It ended as suddenly as it had begun. With his fingers still tangled in the hair at her nape, Aiden pulled away. "Lock the door behind me. Stay away from the window. Stay safe. Please. For me." He kissed her again before releasing her and swinging open the door. When the dog would have charged out ahead of him, he gave a new command. "Blue! *Pass auf!*"

Guard the place.

Guard Lexi.

The slam of the front door went through her like an electric jolt. Her heart might be filled with a million questions about that kiss and who the intruder might be, but she obeyed Aiden's command. She turned the dead bolt, sent up a silent prayer for Aiden's safety, then grabbed Blue by the collar and hurried through the house with him to make sure the back door in the kitchen was also locked and the latch on every window in the house was secured.

She fought the urge to peek through the windows to track Aiden and make sure he was all right. Because she had no doubt that a confrontation with her attacker would turn violent. Instead of making herself a visible target at the windows, she returned to the foyer, leaning against the wall and sinking down onto her haunches in the very spot where Aiden had kissed her with all that raw emotion.

Blue followed her command and sat right beside her, dutifully watching over her in his partner's absence. She hugged her arms around the dog's neck, counting off the seconds until Aiden returned. The minutes dragged on interminably until she heard the sharp knock at the door. "Lex, it's me. Open up."

She raced Blue to the door. The moment she unlocked it, Aiden pushed his way in, pushed her back from the opening, and threw the dead bolt behind him before holstering his weapon and opening his arms, welcoming both Blue and Lexi. She gave a small laugh as Blue nearly pushed her aside to prop his paws up on Aiden's chest. She was content to wind her arms around Aiden's waist and lean her head on his shoulder and snuggle against his strength. His sweater was frosty with the cold, damp air outside, but she didn't mind the cool moisture against her cheek. "Are you all right? Did you see who it was? What did he want?"

He wrapped his arm around her shoulders,

praising Blue and releasing him from the guard command. As the dog dropped down to the floor, Aiden reached around her to dig Blue's Kong out of his jacket and tossed it down the hallway for the dog to chase and play with. "You da man, Blue. Good boy."

Then both arms came around her, his lips settled at her temple, and he exhaled a heavy sigh that stirred through her hair. Something was wrong. He had bad news.

"You didn't see anyone?" Lexi asked, her arms tightening around him. "I didn't imagine him. He was right there on the porch. Blue saw him, too."

"I don't doubt either of you. There are footprints in the snow leading up to the house he tried to cover up. But his escape path was easy to track. They led through your neighbor's yard and out to the street behind us where the snow has been cleared. I'm guessing he had a vehicle waiting and drove off. Without Blue, I have no idea which way he went."

"I knew you should have taken Blue."

"And have that guy double around and come in the back door while I was checking the front?"

She didn't realize how tense she'd become, how isolated she'd felt without Aiden beside her. But she'd had Blue with her, and there wasn't a finer guard dog in all of KCPD. Aiden had been alone. "But if anything had happened to you…"

"Hey. I'm okay." He pulled back just enough to frame her face. His hands were cold on her skin, but his touch short-circuited the downward spiral of her thoughts. "I'm a cop, remember? Routine patrol. I'm just doing my job." He pressed his cool lips to her forehead and pulled her arms from his waist. "Now I need you to do yours. Bundle up and get your kit."

"Good idea." She appreciated the reminder that she was more than a victim here. In fact, she was vital to finding the answers they needed and capturing this freak. She jogged back to her bedroom closet to retrieve her kit and set it on the bench of the hall tree to open it. "I can take pictures and measurements of the footprints. We can match his size against the size of whatever we find on the hotel video."

Aiden put on his insulated jacket and pulled Blue's leash out of the pocket. The dog danced around his legs in anticipation before Aiden ordered him to sit. He put on his harness and attached the leash while Lexi zipped up her coat and tugged on a pair of sterile gloves.

"Wait here." He unlocked the door. "Let me go out first with Blue."

"Why? Is there something else?" Dread sank in the pit of her stomach. "Please, not another dead body."

Aiden squeezed her shoulder, frowning some

sort of apology. "There's a present on your front porch."

"From a delivery service?" Lexi huffed a sigh of relief. Why would that be such dire news? "It's probably one of the gifts I ordered for Levi or Chelsea. This time of year, companies deliver on Sundays."

"I think it's from the man who attacked you."

She pushed past him to look at it. "Why do you say that?"

"Lex." He tried to hold her back, but the dog got in between them, and she got out to the porch before his hand clamped around her arm and pulled her back.

But she'd already seen it. At the edge of the porch. It truly was a gift—not in any kind of plain brown or white shipping package, but a Christmas present wrapped in green-and-red paper and tied up with a speckled beige drapery cord. Speckled pink with faded blood. Beige because all the dye had been leached out of it. The box inside was dented at one end, as if it had been through a brawl. And the tag looked eerily familiar.

"It's from the crime scene, isn't it?" Aiden speculated.

"Looks like it." Her breath gusted out in a cloud between them. "Let Blue do his thing. I'll get my camera."

Lexi scrolled through her photos from Jennifer Li's hotel room and found an image with the exact package. Her attacker had taken this, too. But why return it?

Blue's reaction gave her a reason why.

The dog sniffed at the gift, whined and jerked back. He trotted down to the step below it to sniff it from that angle and had the same reaction, as if something pungent was tickling his sensitive nose. "Probably not a bomb," Aiden guessed, drawing Blue back to his side and giving Lex the okay to snap several photographs. "He's not specifically trained to detect explosives, but he wouldn't shy away from the scent like that. I can call Sergeant Burke if you want. His K-9, Gunny, is trained in explosives detection."

"That won't be necessary." Lexi knelt to take a closer look. She didn't need a dog's nose to detect the heavy use of bleach on the package. That explained the pinkish bloodstains, tainted by the chemical and useless for lab analysis now. This was a taunt, a little gaslighting to undermine Lexi's ability to do her job. A threat meant to assert his superiority over her. The man had physically bested her, and now he thought he could defeat her mentally, too. "This isn't a bomb."

Although her fingers were getting stiff from the cold air, she kept working. She snapped a picture of the gift tag. The *B* in Jennifer Li's handwriting had been scratched out, and a new message had been written in its place.

Try to solve your murder now.

The perp was flaunting the tainted evidence. He was mocking her.

"I think this is the ligature that was around Jennifer Li's neck. The one he took from the crime scene." She untied the cord and carefully set it inside an evidence bag. She opened the box inside and let out an audible moan.

Aiden saw it, too. "Is that…?"

"My stocking cap." It was faded from bleach, but the specks of blood on the embroidered *CSI* letters made her certain it was the one he'd taken from the crime scene. He'd tucked another note inside with her cap.

Be a good girl and give up now. I'll take more than your hat next time.

Lexi tried to remain clinical, despite the chill that was seeping into her very bones. "Why would the killer risk this? Even if he's compromised the evidence, why would he return it to me? There might be something in here we could use. DNA isn't the only clue we can analyze."

"Because he's a creep. He's toying with you. Because he clearly gets off on upsetting you. And hell if I'll let this happen, but he could be setting you up as his next target."

Lexi shook her head. "That doesn't fit his MO.

I'm not a hooker or the other woman. I'm not having an affair. And there were no signs that he stalked the first two victims like this." Now she was really shivering, and it wasn't entirely due to the wintry night air.

"Lex…" She was marginally aware of Aiden and Blue on the steps below her, standing guard between her and the rest of the world. "Bag that stuff and bring it into the house. I feel like we've got eyes on us."

"Still?" Lexi glanced up to see Aiden swiveling his head back and forth, surveying the street. She quickly sealed the contents inside an evidence bag and pushed to her feet. Once she was inside, she held open the door and urged Aiden and Blue to follow.

He closed and bolted the door behind them before sending Blue after his toy and pulling his cell phone from the pocket of his jeans. "Gifting you with a murder weapon is bad. But that's not the part that concerns me."

"What are you talking about?"

"Finding you at a murder scene he's familiar with is one thing…" He paused as his call picked up. "Yes, ma'am. This is Officer Aiden Murphy. Sorry to call at home, but is Detective Watson available? I have a development in a case he's working. I'll hold."

He reached for her, pulling her shivering body

against his chest, hugging her close to his warmth, his strength, his protection.

She understood the point he was making. And it terrified her. "How does this guy know where I live?"

Chapter Nine

Lexi spent the next three weeks fully recovering from her injuries, putting out fires at work, counting the days until her brother came home for Christmas and pretending the domestic bliss she was sharing with Aiden and Blue at her house was somehow real.

Oh, the kisses were certainly real. And Aiden hadn't just made a mockery of her list of items that could make her rethink falling in love with him; the man was a neat freak, he helped around the house, he shared interests with her, and his dog was an adorable sponge for her affection when he was off duty. Plus, Aiden Murphy was in no way, shape or form a lousy kisser—his kisses were exquisite, from the tender, warm touch of his lips on her forehead when he bade her good-night, to the quick press of his mouth against hers when he and Blue were called to duty and he had to leave her at work or at home with one of his buddies from the K-9 corps watching over her house. Lexi had met several of them by now—Sergeant Jedediah Burke and Gunny, Harry Lockhart and Onyx, Albert Logan and Niko, and Enzo Moretti and Blitz didn't seem to mind pulling the extra duty, and they assured her Aiden and Blue had done the same for them and more when asked. She liked his friends, liked that he made regular trips to Chelsea's place to make sure she was feeling secure, liked that he seemed to be having fun prepping for Christmas—sampling the cookies she baked, doing some shopping with her.

When they were away from the specter of Jennifer Li's killer leaving evidence on her front porch and destroying her murder investigation, it almost felt like they were in a real relationship. Like the two of them could really be a couple, and not just friends.

And when Aiden dropped his guard—when he'd had a particularly bad day at work, or one late night when she'd bumped into him coming out of the shower with the towel wrapped low around his hips and his steaming skin leaving little to her imagination—Aiden Murphy most definitely knew how to kiss. Deeply, slowly, thoroughly, until her whole body was a puddle of gooey need and her logical brain couldn't think straight. Or hard and fast and full of promise, demanding an equally frantic response.

But then he'd pull back. Something always seemed to hold him back from crossing the line into being with her. He'd mention her parents or Levi and how much he owed them. Or he'd ask about one of the cases she was investigating and divert her focus to that. He'd made a promise, and keeping that promise meant more to him than his attraction to her did. She could live with that. Damn the man and his code of honor. She loved him, completely, and that was one of the reasons why.

On top of all that frustrated desire, she was a sleep-deprived mess. She'd given up on falling asleep on the couch with him. If she started to nod off during a movie or one of their late-night conversations, she got up and went to bed out of respect for his desire to resist the relationship she wanted with him—that she suspected he wanted, too. But then she'd toss and turn. She'd be cold or she'd hear a noise that made her wonder if the figure in black had returned. She worried that she'd forgotten something in her plans to make Levi's holiday a perfect homecoming for him. Or she'd start thinking about her cases and wonder what she could do differently. How could she make her team work more cohesively? What had she overlooked? Alone, she couldn't shut off all that speculation the way a few drowsy assurances and the haven of Aiden's arms could.

That was why she was sitting in her office right now, rubbing at the weary tension headache coiling between her eyes, watching Ethan

Wynn pace and listening to him vent about the lab's newest hire compromising one of his experiments and jeopardizing a case. "First, she brought me the wrong sample to do the eosin stain on. Started the stain test at her own workstation before I caught the mix-up. Once I got that all straightened out, I asked her to deliver my photomicrographs to Malone to compare to his blood analysis." He huffed in frustration, spun and paced some more. "She was gone twenty minutes. Twenty minutes! I could have had a coffee and taken a sauna by the time she got back to the chem lab."

"Did she say why it took her so long?" Lexi felt compelled to contribute something to turn this from a rant into a conversation.

Ethan stopped and threw up his hands. "She got lost. She had to ask for directions to find Malone's office. She probably went to Daddy to ask for help."

Yep. Lexi's newest hire was Zoe Stockman, Captain Stockman's daughter. If she'd gone all the way to the CSIU office to ask for directions, she really had gotten lost. But Lexi had made her decision carefully, based on Zoe's expertise. Since Zoe was a newly graduated criminalist, Lexi had filled the position with a qualified candidate and saved the department a little money.

But right now, she needed to appease the most experienced member of her team. If he'd been *hungry* for promotion as Dennis Hunt had claimed, then Ethan was probably already nursing a bit of frustration. Having a bad day in his own lab wasn't helping. "Look, I'll advise her to respect your space. But I want to encourage you to handle things a little more diplomatically. Or come to me."

"I've come to you now." He sat in the chair across from her and tapped his finger on the desk before pointing it at her. "You know she only got the job because she's Captain Stockman's daughter. You can't fix incompetence."

"*I'm* the one who interviewed and hired her. On Mac and Dennis's approval. The captain had nothing to do with it." Lexi propped her elbows on the desk and leaned forward, reaching out with a conciliatory gesture. "Zoe's not incompetent. She's new. How many weeks did it take you to learn what was in every storage cabinet and where every division was located? Give her a break. She's a good hire. We need her ready to pick up the workload when Khari goes on maternity leave next month, so we don't get backlogged. Maybe you could be the nice guy and apologize by giving her a more specific orientation tour."

Ethan crossed his arms over his chest and leaned back in his chair. "Not my job. *You're* the boss."

Lexi bit her tongue at the defiant retort. She

swept aside the papers on her desk and jotted a note on her calendar. "Fine. I'll talk to her tomorrow. If we invade your personal space again while we're on the tour, it's because *you* asked for it. I don't want to hear any complaints."

Ethan stood, straightened the front of his lab coat and smoothed his hand over his gray hair. "You get the job done? I won't complain."

He nearly collided with the gray-haired police officer who'd just arrived to knock on Lexi's open door. Ethan retreated into the room, waiting expectantly for Brian Stockman's announcement. "Captain."

"Wynn." Brian Stockman gave him a curt nod.

Lexi stood behind her desk, a zing of adrenaline pumping through her veins and pushing aside her headache. Had he overheard Ethan complaining about his daughter? "Captain?"

"How's my daughter doing? First week on the job." Maybe he hadn't heard the complaints.

Although she spotted the printout for a new case in his hand, Lexi took the time to answer his question, hopefully protecting Ethan from any backlash. "She's learning something new every day, sir. I assigned her to my most experienced criminalist for orientation."

"Good to hear." His proud, paternal smile encompassed both Ethan and Lexi before he held up the assignment sheet. "We've got another DB. Same hotel where Giselle Byrd was found.

The detective who called says the MO is similar. Signs of a fight. Strangulation." He rested his hands on his utility belt and pursed his mouth in a grim frown. "I hope to hell we don't have a serial killer for Christmas."

"Let's not jump to conclusions." Lexi shed her lab coat and hung it on the closet door behind her. "We'll get the facts first. No-Man's-Land is a pretty rough part of town. Anything could happen there."

"Officers have secured the scene and will remain on site while you work." Captain Stockman came into the room and set the printout with the address and other pertinent information on her desk. "I'm not having another Regal Hotel incident."

Lexi almost didn't hear him at first. Her attention was diverted to the Advent calendar hanging on the door. Over half the colorful windows had been opened, one for every day, counting down to Christmas Eve. But for some reason, she'd skipped a number. Instead of today's date, she'd opened tomorrow's window.

Only, since Ethan had been waiting for her to have this meeting first thing when she'd walked in this morning, she didn't remember opening any window on the calendar at all. Not yet. A vague sense of unease washed over her, leaving a trail of goose bumps in its wake. Why did she feel like this mistake was a coded message that was just beyond her ability to understand? Probably because Khari hadn't been able to get any usable DNA off the hair sample from her attacker or from the bleached curtain cord and stocking cap he'd brought to her house. There were too many unanswered questions swirling around inside her head. She'd been the supervising criminalist for nearly a month now, and she was no closer to identifying the killer than she'd been the night she'd been attacked. She didn't need any more mysteries in her life. She needed solid and reliable. She needed her world to make sense.

"Lexi?" the captain prompted.

"Sorry. Got stuck on a thought." She grabbed her coat and smiled at his concern for his people. "We'll be fine, Captain. Thanks." She spared a moment to open today's date and smile at the fun holiday fact behind the door. Then she pushed the door shut on tomorrow's date and put on her coat as he left her office. She picked up the printout and skimmed the information.

"Thanks for not ratting me out to Daddy," Ethan said, his tone apologetic.

"Just doing my job."

He nodded. "Should I gather the team?"

"Please. I want Dobbs there to secure the murder weapon. You. Me." She looked up to meet Ethan's brown eyes. "And Zoe. She needs the field experience."

"Bad call, Lexi. She's not ready."

"She never will be if we don't give her the chance. Besides, I'm the boss. It's *my* call." She looped her bag over her shoulder and nodded toward the door. "Get the team together and meet me in the garage. You can drive."

With a groan that indicated both compliance and displeasure, Ethan jogged down the hallway to alert the others and retrieve his own gear.

Lexi locked the door behind her and pulled out her phone to text Aiden that she was leaving with the team and gave him the address, simply because she'd promised to let him know if she left the lab.

Not to worry. I won't be alone. See you at home. Your turn to cook. :)

His reply made her laugh.

Do you want Chinese takeout or pizza?

Lexi's answer was brief.

Surprise me.

He sent the reply she'd expected. As soon as Blue and I are done with this locker sweep at Central Prep High School, we'll swing by. Don't like you in that part of town.

Where WOULD you like me? She typed the

flirty response, but then backspaced to delete it. Just because they'd been acting like a couple lately didn't mean they really were together. Her heart ached for the boy who hadn't been protected from violence and neglect. She hated that he felt taking care of her was a debt of honor he had to repay her family, but she wouldn't push him into anything he didn't consciously choose to pursue for himself. I'll see you at the hotel or at home. Be safe.

You, too.

THE DOUBLE TIME HOTEL had once been a Kansas City jazz hot spot back in the 1920s. Now, like the rest of the decayed downtown neighborhood, sadly dubbed No-Man's-Land by the members of KCPD who had to deal with the homelessness, gangs, drug use and other crimes in that part of the city that had yet to be reclaimed by a nostalgic younger generation of civic-minded investors, the Double Time had become a hot spot of a different kind. With bars at each of its first-floor windows, it resembled a pawnshop more than a hotel. Most of its Art Deco architecture had either been vandalized or covered up with a corrugated metal sign. And the sad interior hadn't survived the years in any better shape. Mosaic tile floors had been carpeted over, probably in the sixties or seventies, judging by the tiny clouds of dust that marked their footprints as the team carried their gear from the alley where they'd parked across the lobby to the elevator.

Jackson Dobbs wasn't certain the rickety elevator behind the sliding cage door would hold a man of his size, and when he suggested he would take the stairs up to the crime scene on the fourth floor, Lexi and the rest of the team fell into step right behind him. The peach-colored paint in the stairwell was chipped and faded, or covered in graffiti, but at least the steel-and-concrete stairs felt secure beneath their feet.

When they reached the hotel room, Detective Hudson Kramer was there outside the door, waiting for Keir Watson's older brother, Dr. Niall Watson, to finish his preliminary examination of the body.

"Ma'am. Dobbs. Wynn." Lexi shook hands with Hud and introduced him to Zoe Stockman. Then Hud opened his notepad and reported what they knew thus far. "Keir is down in the hotel office with the victim's friend who discovered the body—also in the same business as our vic— trying to get what information he can out of her. Can't tell yet if she's hysterical over finding her friend, or if she's tweaking on meth or some other drug."

"Probably some combination of both." Lexi peered beyond the yellow crime scene tape that crisscrossed the open doorway to see an eerily familiar scene, albeit much less posh than the one she'd processed at the Regal Hotel.

Dr. Watson shifted slightly beside the flame-haired woman's body on the floor, eavesdropping on their conversation as he gathered his instruments. "She's got no ID on her. Blunt force trauma, defensive wounds. Preliminary cause of death is asphyxiation caused by strangulation. The ligature around her neck looks like a section of the curtain cord." The ME pushed his glasses up on the bridge of his nose and stood, diverting Lexi's focus away from the dusty beige drapes at the window. "Based on lividity and liver temp, she's been dead since late last night. I'd say between ten p.m. and midnight." Dr. Watson looked to Lexi. "If you want to come in and get your pictures now, I'm ready to bag her and take her in for a more thorough exam."

Lexi nodded as she gave her team their assignments. "Jackson, you take the bathroom. Ethan and Zoe, you start with the bed and perimeter of the room. I'll be with the vic." Once everyone had gloves and booties on, they ducked beneath the tape and went to work. Detective Kramer stayed with her as the ME stepped out to prepare his gurney and body bag. Lexi snapped general pictures of the room with her camera before zeroing in on the specifics of the crime. "Curtain cord around her neck. Trashed room. Even the position of the body at the foot of the bed is a repeat of Jennifer Li's crime scene."

And she couldn't help but notice that the curtains were open. She took a picture to confirm the observation in case someone tried to play mind games with her later. Because she had a sick feeling that this crime scene was about more than the dead woman. It was about *her*.

Detective Kramer's fingers lightly grazed her elbow, startling her from her thoughts. "Having déjà vu?"

"More than a little." She knelt to take some pictures of the body itself. "If this is a serial killer, there's no pattern in victimology. Giselle Byrd was a Black woman, Jennifer Li was of Thai descent, and this is a Caucasian woman with dyed red hair."

Hud glanced in his notebook. "Her friend called her TNT. Don't know if those are her initials or her personality. Probably a street nickname. The room was rented out by a Paul and Margaret Montgomery. I'm guessing that's not Margaret."

Lexi looked up at the stocky detective. "Montgomery? You're sure that's the name she and her customer used?"

"Yep. Just like the room across the hall at the Regal." He tucked his notepad inside his leather jacket. "We may also have a lead on 'B.'"

"The initials on the gift tags in Jennifer Li's hotel room?"

Hud nodded. "Jennifer was an interior designer. Keir found out that Barton Rutledge III hired her to remodel a lake property he owns. They've worked together for almost two years. A lot longer than it should take to rebuild a deck and put up wallpaper."

"Barton Rutledge, the land developer?" As in thrice-married billionaire businessman? "You think he was having an affair with Jennifer?"

"We intend to find out. His wife alibis him for the night of the murder, but she probably has a billion reasons to lie for him. Rutledge and his attorney are coming in to the Fourth Precinct offices tomorrow for an interview. You want to be there to observe?"

"Yeah." Since some of her key evidence from the Li murder had been stolen, she was both excited and relieved to hear that the detectives had made progress on their end of the investigation. "Maybe there'll be something about him I can connect to the crime scene." She could judge Rutledge's size and build against the man who'd attacked her. Check the color of his hair. And though she expected the real estate mogul had showered and put on cologne between now and the night her attacker had shown up at her house, maybe she could even get close enough to find out if he smelled like bleach. "Text me the time, and I'll be there."

"Will do." The detective eyed the members of her team working around the room, going in and out with gear from their kits or to retrieve what they needed from the van. The ME and another officer were out in the hallway. "I need to join Keir downstairs. You okay if I leave you here? I can't lock out the floor here." He gave her a wry smile. "Not that it did much good the last time."

Lexi pushed to her feet. "That's not on you. Our perp had a passkey and knew where he could hide. It'd be like trying to stop a ghost."

"That's generous of you. My wife had attempts made on her life after she witnessed a murder a year and a half ago. If I was Murphy, I'd be pissed that someone hurt you like that, and I wasn't there to protect you."

She was familiar with the sentiment. "Wow. I'm sorry to hear that. Is she okay?"

"Gigi's great." The detective's expression softened with a smile when he talked about his wife. "It got a jerk out of her life, and her into mine. Sort of an opposites-attract thing, I guess."

"Congratulations."

Could she and Aiden have a happily-ever-after like that once these murders were solved and the threat to her had passed? Would he move out and insist they remain just friends? Or would he be able to drop the alpha protector routine and allow himself to love her?

Hud headed to the door. "I want you in contact with somebody at all times. With your buddies here or one of us. Stay connected to your team. Especially in this neighborhood."

"We will."

With a sharp nod and a promise to let her know about Rutledge's interview, Hud slid out of the way to let Niall Watson in with his body bag.

Lexi assisted, processing what she could without removing anything from the victim herself. But when she moved out of the way to let Dr. Watson and Jackson lift the body, the victim's hair fell away from her face and neck, and a tiny flash of gold caught Lexi's eye. "Wait a minute." She put out a hand to stop them, then gently brushed aside the hair that pooled against the woman's ear. "Oh, my God."

Shaking with the chill that went through her, Lexi steadied her camera and took a photograph. Then she zoomed in and took another of TNT's multipierced ear. Among the diamond chip studs and silver bands dangled a small gold earring, shaped like a sprig of holly leaves with three rubies.

She'd need to get on her computer to make the identification stick in a court of law, but she had no doubt in her mind. "That's the earring Jennifer Li was wearing before I was attacked."

The killer had taken evidence from that crime scene.

He'd added evidence to this one.

What kind of game was he playing with her?

"You okay, boss?" Jackson asked.

She looked up into the big man's eyes, blinked away her confusion and nodded. "I'm fine." She stood back as they zipped up the body bag and strapped it onto the gurney. Niall Watson was watching her, too, although she couldn't read whether he was concerned by her reaction or annoyed by the interruption. "You two go ahead. Jackson, you'll help the ME with the body?" She thanked Dr. Watson for his patience. "I want that earring bagged and sent to my office when you're done."

The ME nodded. Lexi turned to check Ethan and Zoe's progress and found the man who had been ragging on the newbie just that morning leaning in beside her and explaining the merits of one dusting powder over another for picking up latent prints off different surfaces.

"You two okay in here for a few minutes?" She pulled her phone from her pocket. "I need to make a call to Chelsea. Get her started on some research."

With a nod, the reluctant mentor and student went back to work and Lexi headed into the hallway. Once she'd peeled off her sterile gloves and booties and locked them inside her kit, she walked to the relative quiet at the end of the hall-way, as far as she could get from the banging and clanking of the old elevator.

"Hey, Chels," she greeted her friend when she picked up. "You at your computer?"

"Where else would I be?" It was good to hear the friendly eagerness in her friend's voice again. "What do you need?"

"I've got a list."

"No problem. My tea is hot and I'm ready to do your bidding."

"First..." She startled when she heard a screeching whine, followed by a piercing alarm, at the opposite end of the hallway, and a round of male cursing. Poor Jackson. Between the gurney, the ME, his gear and the officer escorting them, they'd probably surpassed the elevator's weight limit and the door had stuck. Using brute force and maybe a tad of claustrophobia-fueled adrenaline, Jackson shoved the door open and stepped out. "Hold on a second." Since the three men seemed aggravated by the stalled elevator rather than being in any real danger, Lexi pushed open the stairwell door at her end of the hallway. When she closed it, it shut out most of the noise behind her. "That's better. Now I can hear you and think."

"Is everything okay?" Some of the good humor had seeped from Chelsea's tone.

For a moment, Lexi considered Hud's warning

about her team staying in contact with someone at all times. Well, Jackson was with the ME—besides, who would dare pick on a man that size? Ethan and Zoe were together. And she was connected to Chelsea via telephone. Plus, Aiden had promised he and Blue were on their way. There wasn't any promise in the world that could make her feel safer than that.

"Just some technical glitches. The elevator isn't working and we're on the fourth floor. I found a quiet spot." Lexi breathed in her calm logic and exhaled her momentary concern. She strolled across the concrete landing to peer out the cracked window with a stunning view of the brick wall across the alley. But with the wintry air whistling through the crack and eroding seams around the frame, she shivered and came back to stand near the railing, where the air was a little warmer. "First, I need you to run a search for any known prostitutes with the initials or nickname of TNT."

It was a quick search. "Oh, yeah." Chelsea read the information off her screen. "Mildred Moss, aka Millie Martin, aka TNT. She's been arrested several times for solicitation, possession of drug paraphernalia, public indecency."

"Does she have red hair? Multiple piercings?"

"In one of these pictures, she's a redhead. Yes, to the piercings."

Lexi nodded at having at least one mystery

solved. "Then that's our vic. Would you forward that information to the ME's office?"

Tap, tap, tap. Chelsea and her computers were a thing of efficient beauty. "Sent. What else?"

Lexi walked down a couple of stairs and sat on the edge of the landing. "I need you to dig deep into Paul and Margaret Montgomery. I'm guessing that's an alias for someone who's stepping out on his wife or girlfriend—possibly with each of these women." It was a classic ruse for a man to register himself and his girlfriend at a hotel, masquerading as a married couple. "I'd really like to identify who was with these women."

"Okay. Looking…looking…" Chelsea gasped with excitement that quickly dissipated. "I've got a Paul Montgomery, deceased. Almost twenty years ago. Looks like an old-money guy. Do you want me to expand my search outside of Kansas City?"

"Not yet." This guy knew his way around KC. He'd been intimately acquainted with the layout of the Regal Hotel, and he knew enough about the Double Time to leave a body where no one would discover it until the following day. And he'd found Lexi's home and knew the residential area well enough to have planned an escape route. "I think our guy's local." The breeze from the window was raising goose bumps beneath Lexi's sweater and CSI vest. She got up to pace the landing, hoping the movement would warm her up enough to finish this phone call. "This may sound like it's coming out of left field, but see if there's any connection between Paul Montgomery and Barton Rutledge III."

"The real estate guy?"

"That's the one."

Lexi hugged her arm around her waist and continued to pace while Chelsea searched. "Um, you're one smart lady. The late Paul Montgomery was Barton Rutledge's father-in-law. Is that significant?"

"You're kidding."

"From his first wife. Paul's daughter was Margaret. Married Barton before he was somebody. She died of cancer six years into their marriage." Clearly, Chelsea was reading again. "Gossip sheet says Rutledge was heartbroken and dated a bunch of women. Moving up in society, drowning his sorrows in the opposite sex. Looks like a different woman at every social event, in just these few pictures that pop up from the newspaper."

Lexi knew she was onto something here. "I suspect he was seeing some of those women outside of social events, too." Jennifer Li, a beautiful, successful businesswoman who had her own reputation to protect, would make an ideal mistress for a man like Rutledge. They shared the same social circles, the same need for discretion. But why kill her? Did he have a history of violence? And how did the two prostitutes fit in? He wouldn't want either of their pictures in the paper with him.

"There's more." Chelsea interrupted Lexi's speculation. "Looks like Paul Montgomery didn't approve of the philandering, threatened to block the inheritance from his daughter's estate. So Rutledge settled down and married wife number two. That lasted about a year before Rutledge started hitting the gossip columns again. Divorced two years later. The rumor mill quieted down a few years ago when he married his current wife, Mandy."

Lexi didn't believe it. "I wonder how long he's been cheating on her, too."

"I doubt a man with that track record could be faithful," Chelsea agreed. "Do you think he's the killer and the man who attacked you? Maybe he got rid of Ms. Li to keep his wife from finding out."

"Or Mrs. Rutledge did know, and she gave him an ultimatum. Pick her or the mistress." Maybe all of this mess was Barton Rutledge cleaning up his affairs to keep his wife happy.

"Although, ew. That's kind of gross to use a father-daughter alias to hide your affairs."

"He's probably thumbing his nose at his father-in-law by cheating under his name." Lexi resumed her pacing. "Be sure you forward all this to Detectives Kramer and Watson. They're interviewing Rutledge tomorrow."

"I'll put it all in a neat and tidy report for them. Anything else?"

"One last thing." Lexi literally crossed her fingers that she was on the verge of finding their murder suspect. "I need you to get into the Double Time Hotel's records from a month ago and tell me if Paul Montgomery rented the room where Giselle Byrd was killed."

Chelsea typed. She waited.

"No."

"Barton Rutledge?"

"Neither." Chelsea sounded apologetic. "Giselle Byrd rented the room."

Not the answer she'd been hoping for. Frowning, Lexi paused at the top of the stairs. "I thought I was onto something. If we could identify this Paul Montgomery, confirm that it's Barton Rutledge or someone else, we'd have a suspect to connect to all three murders. Why use Giselle's...?"

Lexi heard the door creak open and turned a split second before a man in a black hoodie and stocking mask charged across the landing and gave her a hard shove.

She screamed. But that split second gave her enough time to snatch at the railing. Her phone flew from her hand and clattered down the stairs. Her arm jerked in its socket before she lost her grip, but she'd altered her momentum enough to shorten her flying crash. Winding her arms around her head, she hit her hip hard about half-way down before somersaulting to the bottom of the stairs. She landed with a painful jolt on her hands and knees. Nothing broken. No blood this time. But she was too dizzy and bruised to get to her feet.

"Lexi!"

She heard Chelsea shouting her name over the phone. Her connection. *Stay connected to your team.*

"Lexi! Are you okay? Answer me."

Lexi crawled toward her friend's voice. She found her cell in the far corner of the midpoint landing and picked it up, rolling over onto her bottom and leaning against the back wall. Air rushed back into her chest with a painful gasp. She tilted her head up to watch the eerily familiar figure in black at the top of the stairs looking down on her. He reached into the pocket of his loose black trousers and pulled out a long coil of thin rope. Lexi swallowed hard. Curtain cord, if she wasn't mistaken.

The moment he took a step toward her, she raised the phone to her ear. "Call Aiden. *He's* here."

"Oh, my God! I'm dialing him now." She heard the frantic, garbled sound of Chelsea talking on another line.

The black figure took another step. He tugged

the cord between his hands, then pulled it into a loose slipknot. "Find Hud and Detective Watson. Jackson. Ethan. Anybody. I need help."

Where was her team? Didn't anyone hear her scream? How thickly insulated were these walls? Lexi flattened her back against the cinder block wall, getting the leverage she needed to push herself to her unsteady feet. Getting her face smashed into drywall plaster had been painful enough. If he got his hands on her again, there would be a far different outcome if her head hit any of this concrete or steel.

And she could already imagine that cord constricting around her throat.

"He's already in the building." Chelsea sounded breathless but succinct as she shifted from one call to the other. "Where are you?"

Another step. She slid along the wall, wondering if she was steady enough to beat him down to the next landing and out onto the third floor. "West stairwell. Tell him to hurry."

The hooded figure just kept coming, one slow step at a time. He was enjoying his advantage, savoring her stress, probably reliving her fear and helplessness from his first attack.

And then a door slammed open somewhere below her. "Lex!"

Aiden.

"Up here!" she shouted back. "Between the third and fourth floors!"

She heard footsteps charging up the stairs, men harping out logistical orders and agreements as they approached.

The figure in black hesitated.

Aiden was talking to Blue the whole way, pumping up the dog's formidable energy. "KCPD! I'm sending a dog up."

Her would-be attacker's body language changed. He stuffed the cord back into his pocket. His dark eyes glanced up, glanced down, looked at her. *Not so tough when it isn't just you and a lone woman, are you, buddy.*

She recognized the scrabble of Blue's claws as the dog bolted up the stairs ahead of the running footsteps.

Adrenaline surged through her, chasing away the aches and fears long enough for her to meet those dark eyes behind the stocking mask. She shook her head. "You don't want to meet my friends."

Blue was close enough to hear him panting with excitement now.

Cursing on a voiceless huff of breath, the man hurried up the steps and slipped out into the hallway just before Blue came charging around the corner of the landing below her. Aiden and Hud were a flight of stairs behind the dog, taking them two at a time.

"Lex!" Aiden shouted when he saw her. "You okay?"

Nodding, she sank onto the top step and waved them on, indicating she was all right.

Aiden stopped, cupped her jaw and tilted her face up as Hud raced past. His nostrils flaring with each breath, he stroked his thumb across her lips. "Did he put his hands on you?"

She wound her fingers around his wrist, briefly linking them together. "He pushed me down the stairs. But it wasn't a free fall. I'll be fine." She remembered the image of the man preparing the cord to strangle her, too. Her fingertips dug into the muscles of his forearm. "I'm glad you came when you did."

"Murph!" Hud Kramer waited at the door above them. Blue was scratching like mad at the landing door. "Do I let him out to go after the guy?"

"Wait." Lexi tugged against Aiden's arm and stood. "I have people up there. Don't let Blue hurt them."

Aiden whistled. "Blue! *Hier!*" Blue whined, reluctantly leaving the door and trotting down the stairs. Aiden hooked Blue's leash to his harness and shouted up to the detective. "Go! Find that bastard. We'll be right behind you." He holstered his weapon and slipped his arm around Lexi's waist, drawing her to his side. "Can you walk?"

Lexi nodded, clinging to his belt as they went up the steps. Although she felt the bruises as his hip pressed against hers, she was glad to have his strength and sure balance to cling to. "I want to check on my team. I need to finish processing the scene. I need to find answers."

"What did I say about being alone?" he chided, pressing a quick kiss to her temple as they climbed to the fourth-floor landing.

Lexi's eyes widened as she remembered the phone in her hand. "I wasn't alone." She put it up to her ear. "Chels, you still there?"

"I'm still here. Are you okay?"

She turned her cheek to Aiden's shoulder. "I am now. Thank you."

Aiden leaned in to share his thanks, too. "I owe you one, Chels."

"You two are bad for my blood pressure. Just kiss and be happy. I'm hanging up."

After the call disconnected, Aiden paused with his hand on the doorknob. Blue danced around their feet, probably wondering why they'd given up the chase.

Lexi tilted her face to Aiden's. *Just kiss and be happy.* "If only it were that simple."

"I know." He brushed a wavy tendril off her cheek and tucked it behind her ear. By the time he'd dipped his lips to hers, she was stretching up to meet his kiss. It was quick. It was perfect. They shared comfort and passion and even a little frustration, and then it was over. Aiden palmed her hip and moved her behind him as he released her to pull his gun again. "Stay behind me until I give the all clear."

Lexi braced her hand against the back of his protective vest and moved right with him as he and Blue entered the hallway. He quickly checked every access point before moving down the hallway.

They hadn't passed three doors when Hud came out of the opposite stairwell beside the elevator. He grumbled a curse as he holstered his weapon. "I lost him. Kicked in every door on this floor when no one answered." He strode down the threadbare carpet, meeting them in front of the crime scene tape. "I've got two uniforms clearing the stairwell all the way to the roof and down to the lobby. This guy's a chameleon. Either he can blend in with a crowd or he's got multiple escape routes mapped out before he does anything."

"Or both," Aiden conceded, holstering his weapon. "Maybe blending in *is* his escape plan."

"Then what does he do with all those black clothes?" Lexi wondered.

Aiden pulled her up beside him. "A loose jacket with big pockets? A bag stashed close by?"

"Can Blue sniff out something like that?"

"If he had a relatively fresh scent sample to compare it with."

Lexi ducked beneath the crime scene tape. "Ethan? Zoe?"

"Boss lady." Ethan hurried across the room and swallowed her in an unexpected hug that pinched her sore shoulder. His breath gusted in her hair, and she realized he was breathing hard.

"Are you okay?" she asked as she pulled back.

Zoe stepped in beside Ethan, looking equally concerned. "When I heard you scream, I thought the worst. I was never so glad to see Ethan walk back through that door."

Lexi looked up into Ethan's dark eyes. "You left her?"

He raked his fingers through his gray hair, leaving it in a mess. "We needed a bigger evidence bag for the drapes. I never made it down to the van. I heard your scream, too. I thought it was Zoe. I've never run that fast before." That explained the heavy breathing and frantic concern.

Aiden walked up behind Lexi. "Neither of you saw anything?"

Ethan shook his head. "The hallway was empty when I got up here. I had her lock the door behind me. I figured she'd be safer that way."

Zoe nodded. "I didn't unlock it until he pounded on the door."

Aiden turned to Hud Kramer, who hovered in the hallway just outside the room, updating his partner on his cell phone. "You said there were guests—tenants?—in some of these rooms?"

Hud ended the call and gave a curt nod. "I'll get names and contact information and run them against the guests in the rooms next to Jennifer Li's at the Regal Hotel. I'll keep my eye open for any sort of go bag or dump site. Maybe our chameleon is hiding in plain sight as an innocent bystander."

Blue was sniffing the floor, circling around one way and then the other, his nose touching every surface his short leash allowed him to reach. Agitated by something, he probably was picking up the scent of the man on the stairs here in the room where he'd killed TNT.

Blue was warm to the touch as Lexi reached down to pet him. "We'd better get him out of here before he contaminates anything."

Aiden wrapped his hand around Lexi's upper arm, urging her to come with them. Out in the hallway, he gently turned her arm, pointing out the red-and-violet bruise already forming on her wrist. "Damn it, Lex. Your job is not supposed to be the dangerous one." He trailed his fingers down the sleeve of her sweater to capture her hand. "But these crime scenes—it isn't about murder. Not anymore."

She knew what he was going to say. Knew it in her bones. And it terrified her. "It's about me."

Chapter Ten

Aiden pulled his truck into Lexi's driveway and parked. While he was glad to see the Christmas lights he'd installed with a timer had come on as planned, illuminating her entire front porch and some of the front yard, and adding another level of security to the place, he wasn't thrilled to look across the cab of the truck to find Lexi sagging against the seat, staring out the side window into the night.

At first, he thought she'd fallen asleep on the ride home from the lab, since those had been about the quietest twenty minutes he'd ever spent with her in his life. But the lights from the dashboard provided enough ambient light in the truck that he could see her reflection in the passenger-side window. Her pretty green eyes were open, staring through the glass at nothing in particular. That meant she was deep in thought. Either she was processing all the information she and her team and Detectives Kramer and Watson had gathered on the three murders and multiple assaults on her—searching for answers, trying to make logical sense out of a senseless situation—or she was assigning blame, to herself, most likely, for missing a clue that could have captured the killer before he'd had the chance to strike again. What could she have done differently to find the killer, prevent more murders, and keep her and her team safe when they went out to investigate the crimes?

The Lexi he knew had always been hard on herself. She wanted people and cases to line up in a neat sort of organization, so that she could predict outcomes and know who and what she could rely on.

This killer in black who'd come after her three times now had changed the rules, made things personal and far less predictable. She understood that Levi's job was a dangerous one, but she coped by making the world he was coming home to as familiar and predictable as possible. She understood that the feelings she had for Aiden were reciprocated, but she accepted that he wasn't ready to act on those feelings. She was probably feeling a little out of control, a little helpless, because she was used to fixing things and finding answers and speaking truths—and nothing about this past month, from her promotion to tonight, with her attacker coming after her and eluding them yet again, gave her the logic, predictability and security she craved.

Every cell in Aiden's body wanted to reach across the truck and pull her into his lap. He wanted to kiss her until her turbulent thoughts were focused solely on him, and bury himself so deep inside her that the only promise that mattered was the one made between two bodies, two hearts that loved each other.

Just kiss and be happy.

Could the answer really be that simple? What about his promise to Levi and his debt to Leroy and Lila? Thus far, he'd done a lousy job of keeping Lexi safe. He always seemed to be a step behind, as if the killer was closer to Lexi than even he was. How did he get ahead of this creep without taking leave from his own duties to be with her 24/7? And would Lexi really put up with that? What about the friendships he treasured with Levi and Lexi?

Could he trade one kind of happiness for another without the consequences of ruining both?

Her soft sigh filled the quiet truck. "Only one of us gets to brood at a time." She turned to face him. "What are you thinking over there?"

"That I need to get you into the house ASAP. Put a hot meal in you and get you to bed."

Her eyes flashed at the double meaning in those last words. "Don't get a girl's hopes up."

Yeah, a clever and flirty remark like that didn't help his resolve. Although, when he'd seen the blood on Lexi's face Thanksgiving night, and the bruises on her arms this afternoon, he had a hard time remembering what that resolve was. The thought of losing Lexi hurt a hell of a lot worse than losing his relationship with the Callahan family. After all, what was the point of them saving his life if she lost hers?

He had to tear his gaze from the concerned questions that filled hers more the longer he waited to speak. Instead, he made a quick visual sweep of the yard. No new footprints in the snow, no extra shadows lurking near the house. "I think you're mentally and physically exhausted."

"I am a little tired," she admitted, which was a huge concession that probably meant she was dead on her feet. "It took us a while to log in all that evidence, get it into storage and write up the processing assignments for tomorrow's staff meeting."

"That could have waited until tomorrow morning. Or you could have delegated making the assignments," he suggested.

She pushed herself away from the headrest to pick up her bag and loop it over her shoulder. She glanced back at the dog sitting in the cage behind them. "I'll delegate my responsibilities when you delegate Blue's training."

Aiden chuckled. Infallible logic, as always. "Fair enough." He flipped the collar of his jacket up around his ears and climbed out. He retrieved Blue and met her at the hood of the truck. Since her steps were dragging, he slipped his arm around her waist and urged her to lean against him as they walked up onto the porch and unlocked the front door. "Why don't you take a hot shower and put on your pj's while I give Blue an outing and start a late dinner for us."

She dropped her bag on the bench of the hall tree and shrugged out of her coat. "I'm not hungry. But help yourself to whatever you want." She patted her chest to encourage Blue to prop his paws up on her while she stroked his head and flanks. "Don't forget to feed this guy. He gets an extra treat for chasing the bad guy away today."

"Lex…"

She pushed Blue back to all fours and reached over to pat Aiden's chest, petting him like the damn dog. He supposed the more he kept insisting a relationship with him was a bad idea, the less she was going to try to change his mind. "Maybe I will take some hot soup. Or an omelet. Something simple. I like your idea of the hot shower."

Thirty minutes later, Blue was noshing on a rawhide on the rug in the living room. Aiden had had time to put away his gun and protective vest and change into jeans and a sweater. He'd chopped the veggies and set out everything he'd need to throw together an omelet as soon as Lexi joined him.

But the water in the shower was still running.

Thirty minutes? The water had to be cold by now. A vague sense of unease put his senses on alert. He knew Lexi had been exhausted. Had she fallen asleep in there? Had she made it to bed but forgotten to turn off the water?

Aiden set down the forks and plates he'd gathered. When Blue picked up on his tension, he ordered the dog into his kennel, giving his partner the unspoken signal that he was off duty for now. If Lexi was asleep, she didn't need an excitable dog jumping on the bed to see if she was okay.

But Aiden was damn well going to check it out. He hurried through the house to Lexi's bedroom and knocked on the door. When there was no answer, he nudged it open to find the lamps on, her flannel pajama pants and long-sleeve T-shirt folded neatly atop the quilt, and the bed undisturbed. "Lex?" he called out. "Everything okay?"

Maybe she couldn't hear him over the running water. He went to the bathroom door and knocked. "Lex?" No answer. The tiny hairs at the back of his neck prickled to attention. "I'm coming in."

The closed-in room was foggy with steam, and the scent of milk and honey shampoo that meant Lexi to him filled his sinuses before the steam dissipated into the bedroom and he was left with a sudden chill. "Lex? You know I worry when you don't answer me."

The water continued to run. Aiden inched toward the ivy-patterned shower curtain. As he moved closer, he heard another sound. A sniffle. A shuddering gasp.

"Ah, hell." Aiden pulled the curtain back to find Lexi hugging her arms around herself, leaning against the white tile as the cold water splashed over her. She was crying. Shivering beneath the cold water and crying. "Anything but that, baby. Anything but that."

He reached into the shower and shut off the water, not caring that his clothes got wet. "Lex? Do you hear me?" Was she in shock? Was this some kind of emotional breakdown? Exhaustion claiming her mind and body? "I'm going to touch you, okay?" He grabbed the towel off the rack beside the tub and stepped into the pooling water. He wrapped the towel around her slim, naked body and pulled her away from the wall. "I've got you, baby. I've got you."

She caught the corners of the towel and crossed them in front of her, turning into his chest with a loud sob, pressing her face into the juncture of his neck and shoulder. "That woman today is dead because of me." Her voiced sounded raw, and he wondered how long she'd been in here crying.

He tightened his arms around her, rubbing his hands up and down the towel, willing his body heat and the raspy friction of the terry cloth to warm her skin and chase away the chill. "That's not on you," he assured her, turning his cheek into the fragrant waves of her dripping hair. "This guy has fixated on you. But he's the only one responsible for anyone getting hurt." He spied the purplish bruise on her pale shoulder, probably from today's fall, and lowered his head to gently rest his lips against the injury. "We'll get this bastard. You'll figure it out. Blue and I will take him down. No one else is getting hurt."

"How am I going to figure it out? He steals evidence. He destroys it. He adds things that don't belong to throw us off track and show that he's smarter than us." The only warm thing about her were the tears that trickled from her skin onto his. He pulled her impossibly closer, his sweater and T-shirt wet enough to feel the soft swells and frigid points of her breasts pushing against his chest. "He's trying to gaslight me—closing curtains that should be open, disappearing into thin air—and I'm worried he's succeeding. I pride myself on being smart, on thinking logically. But with him... I can't."

Lexi shivered violently against him and Aiden shifted their positions to hook his hand behind her knees and lift her into his arms. He stepped out of the tub and carried her into the bedroom, where he set her down beside the bed briefly enough to pull back the covers, toss aside his sodden sweater and shirt, and toe off his squishy shoes. Then he lifted her onto the bed and crawled in beside her, pulling the sheet, blanket and quilt up over them both. He wrapped his body around hers and pulled her to him like a second skin, and they lay together like they had those first few nights they slept on the sofa.

"You're going to be okay, Lex. You're just having a bad day. You'll come out stronger on the other side."

The shivering gradually subsided, and she shifted her position slightly, finding the sweet spot on top of him where the crown of her hair nestled beneath his chin and her legs tangled with his. "You always say the right thing. Except..."

His body responded as it always did to her clingy softness and sweet scent. How close could a man get to everything he always wanted and still deny himself? He knew what Lexi wanted to hear, and he knew how badly he wanted to say it. But he'd promised Levi.

Stay close to Lexi. Keep an eye on her. Help her out even when she thinks she can do it herself.

You be what she needs when I can't be there for her.

He'd shaken Levi's hand. They'd slapped each other's backs in a bro hug. He'd vowed to always be there when Lexi needed him.

What about what Aiden needed?

After several minutes of blissful torture, as the temperature between their bodies beneath the

covers rose and encompassed them in a fever-
ish heat that sped his pulse and made his jeans
uncomfortably tight with want, Aiden thought
Lexi had drifted off to sleep. But the moment he
tried to shift to a less intimate position, her palms
flattened against his shoulders. "Don't leave me."
She dragged herself up his body until her face
hovered above his. The lamps were still on, giving him a clear view of the puffy skin around
her red-rimmed eyes. But those beautiful eyes
themselves were dark with desire. "I know my
love isn't what you want. I know that what we
already share is precious, and that changing that
is a risk. But I need you right now. To stay with
me. To be with me—"

Aiden tunneled his fingers into her damp hair
and pulled her lips down to his, claiming them
in a reckless kiss. He tongued the seam of her
lips and urged her to open for him. And when
that sexy little moan of desire hummed in her
throat, he speared his tongue into her mouth and
tasted her answering heat. She welcomed him
with passion and tenderness, sliding her tongue
against his, angling her mouth to give him access
to every supple curve, every mysterious hollow.
As they feasted on each other's mouths, her fingertips dug into his shoulders, clinging to him
like a lifeline.

He slid his hands over her bare back and the
flare of her hip. And when he ran into the bar-

rier of the wet towel, he tugged it from under the covers and tossed it aside before bringing his hand back to squeeze the perfect curve of her bottom and anchor her moist heat firmly against the zipper of his jeans. Lexi squirmed against him, pushing her knees apart and dropping them on either side of his thighs, aligning them perfectly together.

This time, Aiden was the one who moaned, and Lexi's lips traveled across the angle of his jaw in search of the source of that guttural sound of frustrated need. Her teeth grazed across his chin and Adam's apple, eliciting tremors of excitement deep within him. He arched his throat, giving her access to taste and torment him, while he skimmed his hands up and down her back, learning every inch of soft skin, of sleek muscle. He played with the tendrils of damp hair that curled around his fingers at her nape, spanned the width of her slim waist. He palmed her butt and hooked his thumbs into the creases of her thighs, sliding against her skin until he found the slick heat of her desire. He pressed his thumb against that sweet bundle of nerves, and she buried her face against his neck, her knees squeezing his thighs.

"Aiden," she gasped. "I want... Can you...? Can we...?"

God, how he wanted her. She was generous and beautiful, a sexy mix of strength and vulnerability. His need for her was potent. How could he deny her anything? How could this be wrong when being with Lexi made it feel like everything that had ever been missing in his life was right here in his arms?

He rolled her over onto her back and recaptured her mouth with his. He slid his thigh between hers and her back arched, her body answering every touch he offered, his body craving every eager response. Her breath gusted against his cheek as she pulled away from his kiss to focus on unhooking his belt buckle and finding the snap to his jeans. "One of us has on too many clothes."

Desire surged through him like a freight train, and he caught her wrists before the choice in what happened next was taken from him. His chest heaving in deep breaths against hers, he stretched her arms above her head and wrapped her fingers around the top edge of her pillow. He planted a quick kiss on her softly swollen lips and then another, until he could control his body enough to speak.

"How do I come back from this?" He brushed aside a lock of hair that had dried against her cheek. "What if this isn't who we're supposed to be?"

Her green eyes looked up into his as she sighed beneath him. She released the pillow to stroke her fingertips across his lips, both soothing his doubts and arousing his hope. "What if this *is* who we're supposed to be? Who we could be? I know I'm stronger, surer of myself and the rest of the world, when I'm with you. And I think you feel more grounded, more secure, when you're with me."

He nodded. "I don't want to lose that."

She stroked her palms across the stubble on his jaw and held his face between them. "I will always be here when you need me." She echoed the words he'd often said to her. "No matter what happens tonight."

Suddenly, Aiden knew there was no turning back. Their friendship had become something more a long time ago. Being with Lexi now, like this, was merely the expression of the bond they shared. He touched her hair again. "Promise me you'll have no regrets?"

"With you? Never."

And then there were no more words. Aiden shed the rest of his clothes and rolled on the condom from his wallet. Her arms wrapped around his neck and her hands skimmed against his hair as he settled between her legs and pushed inside her. Because of her bruises and emotional catharsis, he moved slowly and tenderly with her. Then, because she was Lexi, because she wasn't afraid to demand what she needed from him, because he could no more deny her than he could stop breathing—he claimed her mouth. He kissed her breasts. She wrapped her legs around his waist and lifted herself into his driving thrusts until she cried out his name and arched against him. He could still feel the aftershocks of her release pulsing around him as he came inside her.

After disposing of the condom and splitting an energy bar and glass of milk to compensate for missing dinner, Aiden snugged his arms around Lexi and pulled her on top of him again, where he knew she'd fall asleep and get the rest she needed.

"Thank you for giving me tonight," she whispered drowsily against his chest.

"Not a hardship for me, Lex," he assured her, stroking his fingers through her hair. "I wanted it, too."

"I love you, Aiden Murphy."

With that burden weighing on his mind, he tucked the covers securely around them and lay awake in the darkness long after she drifted off to sleep.

LEXI WOULD HAVE thought having Aiden with her 24/7 would be a good thing.

But having moody, brooding Aiden with her was a little like having a damaged tooth throbbing in her mouth. With the right kind of attention, and some TLC, the tooth could be fixed, and the pain would go away. Why couldn't that man choose to be happy? She'd always thought she was the brainiac in this relationship, who spent far too much time inside her head. But he could work a problem for hours, days, years, maybe—until he'd assessed all the possible outcomes and made the right choice. But whose idea of what was right was he searching for? Had he lost too much to believe that he'd lose her, too, if he let himself care too deeply? Because she knew he did care.

The man who'd saved her from her own mini-breakdown last night cared.

The man who'd made such glorious love to her last night cared.

The man who kept her demons at bay and held her throughout the night cared.

He could fix a mean breakfast and drive her to work and brood and stand guard, all with that sexy, crooked smile of his. He'd risk his life for her and kiss her until her toes curled and give her everything she needed.

But he wasn't ready to take that leap of faith with her. He wasn't ready to say this was love.

He might never be.

But she would take their unique version of a relationship over whatever twisted thing was going on between Barton Rutledge III and his wife, Mandy.

Lexi had taken Hud up on his invitation to observe him and his partner, Keir Watson, interviewing the real estate mogul and his wife, who had to be at least three decades younger than her white-haired husband. The husband and wife sat with their attorney across the table from Hud and Keir, facing the observation window in the next room, where Lexi stood with her arms crossed, taking in every detail of the couple's interaction as though it was a crime scene.

Mandy Rutledge applied her lipstick in her compact mirror again, dabbing a tissue against the already perfect arc of matte pink. Then she reached over to wipe away the tear that ran down the billionaire's gaunt cheek before tucking the tissue into his misshapen arthritic hand where it rested on copies of Lexi's crime scene photos.

"Your questions are upsetting my husband, Detective Watson," Mrs. Rutledge said.

Keir was unfazed by the accusation. "I only asked if he knew the woman in the photograph."

"Of course he knew her. We hired her to revamp several lake properties for us."

"Shut up, woman. I can speak for myself."

"Don't say too much," his attorney warned.

"Both of you, stop," he ordered, his aging voice still indicating that he was the boss. He raised a gnarled knuckle to wipe away his own tears. Then he lowered his hand to touch one of the gruesome photos of the lifeless woman. "Yes, I knew Jennifer. We met through the lake project, but we became…more."

"You were having an affair with her?" Keir prompted.

He glanced over at his wife, who quickly turned away. "Yes. I've been seeing her for some time."

"Looks like you were planning to see her on Thanksgiving night. The night she was killed."

Hud pointed to a different picture. "She bought a bunch of presents for you, big guy. She was looking forward to seeing you."

Rutledge eyed Hud with contempt, as though being spoken to by the only man in the room not wearing a suit and tie was an insult. He turned to Keir to answer. "I was looking forward to seeing her, too. Jen was such a light. She was so smart, such a good listener. She made me laugh."

Aiden walked up to the window beside her, propping his hands at his waist. "If he says she was good in the sack while his wife is sitting there, I'm leaving."

Lexi couldn't help but grin. "I don't think he cares much about what his wife thinks. Chelsea's research says Mr. Rutledge has a long history of affairs. He marries for money or status. Then, after a while, he steps out, looking for the love he doesn't find at home because that's not what the marriage is about for him."

"Hell. Sounds like my dad." When she glanced up in concern, Aiden shrugged off the bad memories. "On a much cheaper, drunker scale, of course. Patrick Murphy married for a sex partner, a paycheck or a babysitter. I used to hope that he at least loved my mother. But maybe he just didn't have it in him to love."

Lexi reached out to rub his arm, since this wasn't exactly the place to offer a kiss or hug of comfort. Not that she was sure Aiden wanted anything like that from her today. "You're not like your father. You know how to love better than any man I've known. You're too good at taking care of people—of your friends, of Blue, of me—to not have love inside you."

He reached over to briefly cover her hand where it rested on the sleeve of his uniform when the fireworks started in the interview room.

"I loved Jennifer!" Rutledge insisted, shoving the photographs across the table. "Why do you think these pictures upset me? I can't stand seeing her like this."

"Did she threaten to break it off with you?" Hud pushed.

"Had she become a liability you needed to get rid of?" Keir pushed harder.

Rutledge's chair slammed against the back wall as he stood up. "I did not kill her!"

Aiden braced his hands at his waist again. "He's mad enough to throw a punch, isn't he?"

Lexi's gaze went to the man's bony knuckles and twisted fingers. She flinched as she relived the fist coming out of nowhere and cracking her cheek Thanksgiving night.

"He's not our man," she murmured under her breath.

Hud and Keir were on their feet, too.

"Sit down, Mr. Rutledge." That was Hud, circling the table to muscle the suspect back into his chair if he had to.

"Where were you Thanksgiving night?" Keir asked. "In the hotel room across from Jennifer, staying under the assumed name of Paul Montgomery?"

"What? No. I canceled that reservation…"

"Barton." His attorney urged him to sit and be silent.

By the time Rutledge had resumed his seat, he looked more like a confused old man than a powerful business mogul. The old man shook his head. "I was at home with my wife."

Hud remained standing while Keir sat. "Why the change of plans?"

Barton glanced at his wife. Now she was primping her flawlessly styled blond hair into place. "Family gathering. For the holiday. It was last-minute. Mandy arranged it. Typically, she flies home to her family. But I guess, with the snow, her flight was delayed, and so she wanted to surprise me." He glanced back at Keir. "I called Jennifer, told her I'd be late. Or it might even be the next morning before I could get away."

Mandy's compact tumbled onto the table. "You planned to see her anyway?" She snatched it up and tucked it into her purse. "You couldn't give me a whole weekend of your time? After I went to so much trouble?" She stood and headed for the door. "I'm sorry. I find this all terribly upsetting." When she got to the locked door, she spun around to lambaste her husband until Hud could get it open for her. "You never were going to give me a chance, were you? Jennifer. Jennifer. Jennifer."

When Barton didn't even look up at her, she stormed out.

Lexi shook her head, sorting out the answers that would have this all make sense. "Barton Rutledge didn't kill Jennifer Li."

Aiden didn't see it yet. "His heartbreak and anger could be an act."

"Look at his hands."

Aiden curled his own fingers into fists the older man could never make. "He's not our killer."

Lexi squeezed one of those fists and hurried to the door. "I know you're not a detective, but will you follow my lead? Play along with me?" She nodded to the interview room. "Get Hud or Keir to come along after a couple of minutes, too."

"What are you...?"

But Lexi was already out the door, hurrying over to Mandy Rutledge as the blonde stepped out of the interview room.

"Mrs. Rutledge?" Lexi fixed a sympathetic look on her face and extended her hand. "I'm Lexi Callahan from the crime lab. I was watching that interview. Would you like a cup of coffee? Some tea? A chance to sit someplace that's a little quieter?"

The other woman never took Lexi's hand, but she hugged her clutch to her chest and exhaled a grateful sigh. "Yes. A cup of tea would be nice. This whole sordid business and the detectives' veiled accusations have me quite distraught. And no telling what the stress is doing to Barton's heart."

Not to mention the stress of being married to a calculating wife, if what Lexi suspected was true.

Lexi escorted her to the break room down the hall. It wasn't the expansive modern space they enjoyed in the crime lab's memorial lounge. But the yellow brick walls and black vinyl sofa of the Fourth Precinct's third-floor lounge, especially with its glass front wall, should do the trick.

Mandy perched on the edge of the sofa while Lexi opened a tea bag and dropped it into steaming water. "Cream or sugar?" Lexi asked.

Once she'd doctored the tea to Mandy's liking and handed her the insulated paper cup, Lexi poured herself a cup of coffee and sat at the small round table across from her.

"Thank you." Mandy graciously accepted the tea and played with the tea bag before taking a sip. "I know it's the detectives' job to ask questions. But it's just so humiliating to hear my husband spell out that he's been unfaithful to me."

"I can't imagine what that's like," Lexi sympathized. "Sometimes those police officers barrel into a situation and ask questions later. They're hardwired to take action. Me, on the other hand? I like to tiptoe around the crime scene after the fact. Have some quiet time to myself to process and understand what has happened before I start to look for answers." She smiled. "More observing and less action."

"Thank you for saying that. Yes, a little more delicacy would be appreciated in how they handle suspects." Aiden strode in between the two women and poured himself a cup of coffee. Then he went back to the entrance and leaned against the door frame, casually crossing one booted foot over the other, clearly not going anywhere. Mandy set her tea on the table beside her, not too sure about Aiden lingering close enough to eavesdrop on them. "I thought this was a private room."

Lexi smiled at her hero. "He's my armed guard. I've worked three murder scenes this month. I was attacked while I was processing Jennifer Li's murder scene."

"Attacked?"

Aiden held out his coffee cup and pointed to her, catching on to Lexi's informal Q&A session. "You were attacked at the third murder, too. Don't forget that."

Mandy's skin went pale beneath her makeup. "Third murder?" She glanced from Aiden over to Lexi. "I thought we were here because of Ms. Li."

"We are." Lexi chatted on, as if they were discussing Chiefs football or the weather. "There were three murders with the same MO. There was a struggle. The victim was subdued with a blow to the head, then strangled. Or, possibly, the struggle was staged afterward. Three women knocked unconscious or incapacitated. Three women strangled with cord cut from the draperies."

"No, there were only two women." Mandy scooted to the edge of the couch, then erased the contention from her tone and sat back. "I mean, that's what I read in the paper."

"Trust me, I have the bruises to prove there was a third."

Mandy moved to the edge of the couch again. "Barton didn't do it. He didn't kill anyone."

Lexi rose to pour the coffee she hadn't tasted into the sink. "I know he didn't. I saw his hands. He couldn't hold a rope, much less pull it tight enough to choke someone to death. Punching me with a fist would have been unbearably painful. And my attacker didn't cry out. He never said a thing."

"Barton was home with me. All day Thanksgiving. All night."

Hud, Keir, Barton and his attorney were gathered at the door behind Aiden now. "Your husband might have come home on Thanksgiving, Mrs. Rutledge. But were you there?" Lexi asked. "Are you alibiing him just so you have an alibi for yourself?"

"You weren't there when I got home, Mandy," Barton admitted. "You said you were running errands on your way home from the airport, then got stuck in traffic. I was home by myself for three hours—long enough to watch a football game—before you got there." He glanced at his attorney. "When we heard about Jennifer on the news, Mandy offered to cover for me. She said the police were bound to find the connection between me and my mistress."

Mandy shot to her feet. "Why are you being honest now, you idiot?"

"Did you kill Jennifer?"

She shook her head, blaming her husband. "You cheating son of a bitch." Then she turned to Lexi, as if being the only other woman in the room meant she would understand. "He said that he was in love with her and that he was going to leave me. I was going to lose everything. It's one thing to cheat on me." She whirled around to her husband again. "It's another thing to cast me aside like you're trading me in for a new model."

"And the two prostitutes?" Keir asked.

"I'm telling you, there weren't two!" Mandy must have finally realized that she'd already confessed to too much. "I hired Miss Byrd. Told her she was a birthday present for my husband. I was waiting for her when she checked in. I wanted to practice, to make sure I could do it and cover my tracks. Throw the police off, too—have them think they were looking for a serial killer. I was so certain I'd taken care of everything, staged it so it couldn't be solved. How…?"

Lexi looked to Aiden, then to Mandy. "Someone came along after you left and tampered with your crime scene."

A complication she hadn't anticipated. Mandy's shoulders sagged in her Chanel suit. "I want to talk to my lawyer now."

The attorney stepped into the room and took her by the elbow. "That would be wise, Mandy. Remember, you were Mirandized along with Barton when we went into that interview room. I'll do what troubleshooting I can, but for now, just keep your mouth shut."

Mandy walked out the door with him but turned to Lexi one last time. "I didn't kill *three* women."

Hud gestured to the interview room they'd vacated. "Well, let's talk about the two you did."

"She didn't kill three women," Lexi agreed

after they left with the detectives. "After Jennifer Li, she had no need to."

Aiden crossed the room to rub his hand up and down her arm. "What about her accomplice? The man who attacked you?"

"There was no accomplice."

Aiden tossed his cup, then came back to stand in front of her. "You're going to explain this to me, right?"

"We agree that TNT was murdered to get me to that crime scene?"

"Yeah. And?"

"Who would know all the details of the first two murders and be able to stage that scene to look just like the first two deaths? Especially to a trained eye like mine?"

"Another criminalist." He'd been trying to protect her from a stranger, an unknown subject who liked to hurt women. If he could keep the danger away from her home, away from her work, she'd be fine. But the threat was already part of her world. "We've been investigating this like there was one perp. We've got two separate crimes."

The enemy was one of her own.

Chapter Eleven

"Thank you, Mac."

Lexi's boss was shaking her hand in the middle of the crime lab lounge, with most of her friends and coworkers gathered around for their lunch break. "Thank you for proving my faith in you was justified. Two murders solved, and you've barely been running your part of this place for a month."

He released her as several of the others came up to congratulate her. Grayson Malone rolled up in his wheelchair. "Can I tell you how much faster work gets done around here? People aren't looking over their shoulders and second-guessing themselves. You don't give us orders we can't carry out." He squeezed her hand. "Very military-like of you."

High praise indeed.

Khari Thomas was right behind him. She leaned in for as close a hug as her nearly full-term pregnancy allowed. "You're the best, sister. I hardly remember Dennis What's-His-Face anymore."

Lexi smiled. "Thanks for putting the rush on that DNA comparison. Detectives Watson and Kramer are very happy to have the science to back up Mandy Rutledge's confession."

"Just doing my job." Khari grinned. "Not having to worry about anything else while I'm doing it is a pleasure."

Jackson Dobbs patted her shoulder. "Nice job, boss."

Brian Stockman reached in to shake her hand, too. "You resolved the dispute between Ethan and Zoe, which I appreciate. Next thing you know, those two will be dating. Not sure how I feel about a man who looks my age being sweet on my daughter."

Lexi laughed and sought out Ethan and Zoe sitting at a table together with their sack lunches. Zoe's back was to her, but Ethan sat up straight and gave her a thumbs-up.

But as the congratulators began to disperse and the crime lab staff went about fixing their lunches, setting up chess games and joining conversations, a stocky figure wearing a suit and loosely knotted tie appeared at the lounge door and gestured to get her attention. Why was Robert Buckner waving her over? Beyond their introduction a month ago, she hadn't traded more than a polite greeting with the private investigator.

Still, his square face had a stern set to it. Something was wrong. Something to do with Chelsea? Lexi quickly glanced around the lounge. Where was her friend, anyway?

Lexi excused herself from her colleagues and crossed to the door. "Are you looking for Rufus?" she asked about his former partner, just in case she'd misunderstood that he wanted to talk specifically to her.

"No." He closed his hand around her arm above her elbow and pulled her into the hallway. "Could I see you in your office?"

"Sure." He released her when she fell into step beside him. "Is this about an investigation?"

"No." His voice turned gruff with some tightly controlled emotion. "But I need you to handle this. I don't think I'm the right person to do it. Your boss might not appreciate how I'd deal with it."

Now *she* was concerned. "What are you talking about?"

They'd reached her office. She'd left the door open when she'd gone to meet Aiden for lunch in the lounge. He was running late after he and Blue had been called to help with a drug-related traffic stop. And then Mac had come in for a bottle of water and the embarrassing adulation had started.

But now her door stood slightly ajar. She glanced up at Mr. Buckner, and he inclined his head, indicating she enter first.

Lexi pushed open the door and Chelsea vaulted out of her chair and threw her arms around Lexi's neck. "Oh, gosh, Lexi, I screwed up."

"*You* didn't do anything wrong," Buck grumbled from the doorway.

Chelsea shook in her arms, crying. There were no tears, only dry sobs, clueing her in that her friend had been at this crying jag for some time. She mouthed a question over Chelsea's shoulder to the older man. *"What?"*

"Oh. Buck. I'm sorry." She held out a soiled navy blue bandanna that she'd been wringing between her fists. "Here."

He gently pushed the bandanna back into her fingers. "You keep it."

Chelsea hiccuped a laugh. "Right. It's gross. I'll wash it."

She stepped forward as if she wanted to hug him. Buck's arms came out. And then there was an awkward pat on his chest and a squeeze on her shoulder, and the hug never happened.

Chelsea sniffed and tipped her chin up and smiled. "Thank you."

Buck nodded. Then looked beyond her to Lexi. "Take care of her for me."

Lexi nodded as the older man closed the door. After a slight hesitation, Chelsea turned and reached for Lexi's hand. "We need to talk."

"Okay." Lexi settled into the chair beside her friend because she seemed to need the tight clasp of their hands. "What's with you and Buck? That's what I'm supposed to call him, right?"

Chelsea nodded. "I couldn't take it anymore. Dennis came by my computer lab this morning. And when Buck picked me up for lunch, I just... broke down. He gave me his handkerchief, and I blubbered all over the front of his suit."

"Dennis?" Lexi sat up straight, suddenly feeling every bit of grim tension Buck had displayed. "Go back, Chelsea." What did Robert Buckner know that she didn't? "Tell me about Dennis."

Chelsea pulled her hands back to her lap and worked the bandanna between her hands until she could speak. "Dennis has been blackmailing me."

"What?"

"I know he's in trouble for harassing several of us here." But this was something more. Lexi let her friend tell the story the way she needed to, although she was already composing the text to Aiden, warning him that he might have to handcuff her to keep her from committing violence. "But one of my foster home placements..." Lexi frowned as the story took a turn into left field. "It wasn't a good situation. Dennis... A few months ago, he had me in his office." Lexi could already imagine where this scenario was leading, what must have happened to make a relative stranger, yet one who was a former cop, like Robert Buckner, get involved. The tears threatened to start again. "Dennis cornered me. He had his hand up my skirt, and it triggered a flashback from the foster home."

Lexi carefully schooled all the rage from her tone. "What happened?"

"I attacked him."

"You fought back. You defended yourself."

"I assaulted him. I stabbed him in the shoulder with a letter opener, sliced open his hand."

Lexi remembered the unexpected four-day weekend Dennis had taken. She'd had to cover for him and pull extra duty shifts. When he got back, he explained away his bandaged hand and limp arm by some outrageous excuse about his fiancée scratching him during sex—then claiming to have had an accident when he'd been working on fixing up her house to sell it before they moved into his place together.

While she abstractly prayed that Bertie would get a clue and dump him, Lexi stayed focused on the big problem at hand. "He threatened to report you if you don't withdraw your complaint against him?"

"He took pictures. Put the letter opener in an evidence locker. He's going to claim to be the victim and turn it around at his hearing to say we're the ones harassing him. Making up lies about him."

She didn't know Buck well, but she could imagine how an old-school man like that would handle this extreme form of sexual harassment. She'd like to be there if that ever happened.

But she was new-school. And her way would be no less effective. As Chelsea's supervisor and best friend, it was her responsibility to deal with this.

"You have to report him, Chels. He's the one who assaulted you. You had to defend yourself."

"But he's the one with the evidence."

Lexi knew plenty about false, corrupt evidence. "I don't mean to the review board. I mean to the police. Dennis committed a crime. Attempted rape."

Chelsea shook her head. "I can't talk to the police about this."

"Could you talk to Aiden?" She already had her phone out, prepping the text as Chelsea considered it. "I'll be right there with you. If you want me."

Chelsea dabbed her nose with the bandanna and gave one last sniff. "Okay."

Lexi sent the text. She had no doubt the cavalry would be on its way soon.

"You're a good friend, Lexi. Buck said I should come to you. Of course, I couldn't stop crying. He probably just wanted to get rid of me."

"No, I think he was concerned. I still worry about you moonlighting for him, but I think he's a friend. I'm glad he brought you here." She squeezed Chelsea's hand and stood. "I'm glad you talked to me. I promise you—Dennis won't be here tomorrow." She pulled her friend in for one more hug. "Take a few minutes to splash some cool water on your face and regroup. Take however long you need." Lexi headed out the door.

"Where are you going?"

"I'm going to go be your boss right now."

Her confrontation with Dennis Hunt proved to be short and immensely satisfying. She'd already contacted Mac and knew Aiden was on his way. Once she'd laid out how the police were going to be investigating him for attempted rape, witness intimidation and extortion, he'd come up out of his chair.

"What is your problem, Callahan?" She backed out of his office as quickly as she could. But he grabbed her arm and slammed her against the wall, spitting in her face as he cursed her. "You witches are all out to destroy me."

Lexi heard a low growl. The most beautiful sound in the world.

Lexi's words were as succinct as she could make them. "You touch? You go."

Dennis wisely released her, but he didn't immediately back away. He glanced to the left to see Mac, Khari, Jackson, Rufus King, Gray Malone and other witnesses at one end of the hallway. Then he glanced to the right to see Aiden in full protective gear, fighting to hold a lunging, snarling Blue in check. He only had to say one thing to convince Dennis to surrender.

"I can let go of the leash."

BY THE TIME December 23 rolled around, Lexi had begun to relax. She was getting the hang of this supervisor stuff. She still had friends at the lab, and she still had Aiden living at her house, if not sleeping in her bed. They shared meals. They watched old movies and laughed. Aiden was still the model houseguest.

But they couldn't seem to recapture the closeness they'd shared that night she'd been shoved down the stairs at the Double Time Hotel. Confessing her love had pushed her knight in shining armor back into his celibate vow, putting duty and protection before affairs of the heart.

Lexi thought she could handle his decision not to pursue a romantic relationship as long as he was with her. Maybe she had enough love for both of them.

But it whittled a little bit away from her heart each day. It made her sad that Aiden didn't seem to believe they could be both best friends and soul mates—that he'd rather close off his heart than make a mistake that might hurt her or cost him the family he needed so much.

Until they could confirm that Dennis was behind the assaults on her—an accusation that he denied as vehemently as he denied the other charges against him—Aiden had vowed to remain her round-the-clock protector. But since there had been no other incidents, the timing seemed to indicate that the man with the grudge against women was her attacker and had murdered TNT to lure her to the crime scene. Lexi's team hadn't been called to any other homicides, and the lab was getting the chance to catch up on and clear backlogged cases they were working for KCPD, the state police and the Cass, Clay, Platte and Jackson County sheriff's offices.

Meanwhile, Mandy Rutledge had been indicted on two counts of homicide. Dennis was in jail awaiting trial, no longer a cancer impacting so many lives at the lab. Chelsea was smiling again. The crime lab team was gelling in a way that made it a place where everyone looked forward to going to work again. A fresh new fall of snow had made the city pretty again, ready to celebrate Christmas.

Tonight, the lab was running on a skeleton on-call crew like during Thanksgiving, in deference to the upcoming holiday. Lexi was on duty as supervisor and it had been a quiet evening, giving her plenty of time to catch up on paperwork and wrap a couple of presents on her breaks.

Since it had been such a quiet night, she was startled when her phone rang. Captain Stockman was off duty, calling from home to give her the assignment. "Sorry to do this to you, Lexi," he apologized. "Don't know why the criminals don't hole up and stay home like the rest of us when it's cold and snowy like this."

She had her pen and notepad at the ready. "What have we got?"

"Another trip to No-Man's-Land to visit the Double Time again." Lexi chuckled and jotted down the information. "Homicide in Room 519. You be careful."

"It's okay, Captain. I'll have Aiden with me."

"He's a good man."

"Yes, he is." Lexi was already up to get her coat from the closet. "Okay. We'll roll in Aiden's truck and I'll call the team in to meet me there."

"Be safe. And merry Christmas."

"Merry Christmas."

She texted Aiden. Got a call. Homicide. Can I bum a ride with you and Blue?

On my way.

Twenty minutes later, they were pulling into the alley beside the Double Time. Aiden killed the siren, but left his lights flashing—for the illumination as much as for the official presence of law enforcement. Lexi frowned as she peered beyond the trash bins and garbage bags into the shadows. With Blue locked in his cage behind them, panting with excitement at the opportunity to go to work, she had to look in the side-view mirror to see the street behind them. There were plenty of parked cars and music and lights from the bar across the street. But the recent winter storm had driven almost everyone inside. The sidewalk was empty except for the trio of men smoking out on the bar's front stoop. There was some traffic moving along the street, but not much. It was cold. The streets were slick, and the hour was late.

"Where's the CSIU van?" They'd had to spare a few minutes to give Blue the chance to relieve himself and put his protective vest on him. "I figured they'd be here before us."

She pulled out her phone to text Ethan, Shane and Zoe, and ask them what their twenty was. She looked across the truck to Aiden in his KCPD jacket, gloves and stocking cap. He was surveying their surroundings, too. But where she'd been curious, his blue eyes were narrowed in suspicion.

"What is it?" she asked. His wariness filled the cab's warm air and put her on alert, too.

"Where are the black-and-whites to secure the scene? Who called it in?" He reached across the seat to squeeze her hand. "Stay put. I'm going to check things out."

He opened the door. A blast of chilled air rushed in as Aiden left her.

And then the nightmare began.

She heard a soft impact sound, like leather

gloves clapping together. Then Aiden swatted his
thigh. If it wasn't zero degrees out, she'd think
he'd been stung by a wasp. Then she heard the
jolt of electricity buzzing through the air and
Aiden cursed. By the time he was shaking and
collapsing to the asphalt, Lexi had unhooked her
seat belt and was crawling across the center con-
sole. "Aiden!"

She'd processed enough of the barbs that de-
livered a powerful electric jolt to know that he'd
been tased. Blue barked wildly behind her, seeing his partner pass out and fall like that.

But Lexi never made it out of the truck. She
never got the chance to see if Aiden was hurt. If
he'd hit his head on the truck or the pavement or
worse. Just as she was stepping out the door, a
black-gloved hand pointed the Taser at her. She
sank back onto the driver's seat, feeling the chill
of the wintry air and something even colder deep
beneath her skin.

The figure in black. Hooded. Faceless behind
his mask. Always one step ahead of her. But
someone she knew. Someone she trusted. She
knew that now. She quickly scanned through her
memory, lining up body shape and height of the
people she knew to this man. Two working legs,
so not Grayson. Not big enough to be Jackson.
Average height. Average build. Average in every
way except for the weapon he held in his hand.
He switched the Taser to his left hand, keeping

it trained on her as he stooped down to unholster Aiden's Glock. He pointed the gun at her, too.

He made his first mistake. This time he spoke.

"Get out of the truck and come with me. Or I'll shoot the dog." Blue was going nuts behind her, shaking the truck as he jumped against the walls of his cage. Would anyone in this part of town respond when they heard a dog bark like that? Or would they duck their heads and shy away from the obvious threat he represented?

Second mistake. He'd threatened Blue.

When Lexi didn't immediately move, he aimed the gun at Aiden's head. "How about I shoot the boyfriend?"

Third mistake. He'd threatened the man she loved.

The enemy in her midst.

"Hello, Ethan."

Chapter Twelve

By the time Ethan had unlocked the door to Room 519, Lexi knew he'd rerouted the rest of the team to a different address and planned to meet them there within a reasonable time frame. They were all on call, coming in from different locations, dates and family events. Just like after the murder at the Regal Hotel, no one would question them arriving separately at different times. Only Captain Stockman had this address and knew where Lexi had been dispatched. But with Ethan calling the shots, there'd be some confusion and miscommunication before he figured out that Lexi was missing.

By the time he unlocked the door, she also knew he intended to kill her.

Ethan closed the door behind him and nudged her toward the foot of the bed with the barrel of Aiden's gun. "As much as I want you to suffer, I have a plan and a schedule to keep."

Lexi turned to face him and the gun. "What

about Aiden? That Taser won't render him unconscious forever."

"I gave him the maximum voltage. He'll be out anywhere from ten to thirty minutes." He pulled a length of cord from the pocket of his black pants, which she now realized fit so loosely to hide the khaki trousers he wore underneath. That explained his ability to disappear into a crowd, or even reappear at a crime scene without anyone ever noticing. A quick-change artist. Those pants probably doubled as a bag to wrap the rest of his black gear in. Drop it inside a CSI kit or large evidence bag, and no one would be the wiser. "My goal wasn't to kill him." He was careful to keep his hood and stocking mask in place as he circled around her. Smart. That way he wouldn't accidentally leave a stray hair behind. Other than the one she'd raked off him at the Regal Hotel when she fought with him. "I want Aiden to find you. Dead, of course. The two of you are just too precious, pretending to be friends when I'm sure you're shagging each other, living together the way you do. The hypocrisy makes my stomach churn."

Lexi mentally tried to visualize how many minutes it had taken them to ride up the hotel's rickety elevator and get to 519. Five? Ten? What if Aiden came to sooner than Ethan expected and found her alive? If she could stall him long enough, it would give Aiden enough time to rescue her. If she could figure out how to get that gun and Taser away from Ethan, it would give her more than a fighting chance to survive this vendetta against her.

She realized Ethan had his CSI kit in the room. Everything had already been staged like the other crime scenes. Furniture tipped over, a dent in the wall—all signs of a violent fight. He reached into his kit and pulled out a long narrow bag with a knifelike object in it.

"What's that?" Lexi asked, sitting on the edge of the broken-down mattress. With everything else topsy-turvy in the room, she doubted wrinkling the bedspread would make any difference.

"Dennis Hunt's DNA." He pulled the blood-stained item out of the bag. A letter opener. Was that the weapon Chelsea had used to defend herself against Dennis? "Thanks to you, he's already a suspect in everyone's mind. He makes the perfect patsy to take the fall for me."

"Why, Ethan? I know you didn't kill those first two women. Why did you attack me at Jennifer Li's murder?"

"Because I was pissed off!" He whirled around, stabbing the letter opener into the mattress beside her. When she jumped out of the way, he pushed her onto the bed and put the blade to her throat. She felt the burn of its sharp edge nicking her skin. The gun ground into her stomach. "You got everything I wanted. Everything I deserved."

She shook her head, afraid to antagonize him, but knowing she needed time for help to come. *I will always come when you need me.* Aiden's voice echoed through her brain, calming her fear, allowing her to think.

As she tried to avoid both the gun and the knife, her breathing was shallow, so her words came out in a breathless gasp. "You've already screwed up, Ethan. There were no knives at any of the crime scenes. None of the victims were cut."

He laughed, tossed the letter opener into the corner beside the dresser and jerked her to her feet. He shoved her hard, and she stumbled backward until she hit the wall. "No, but the victims all fought back. They all had defensive wounds. This time, the victim grabbed the letter opener to fight off her attacker. He wrested it from her, and she died anyway. You don't know everything, boss lady."

"There were no guns, either. How are you going to explain Aiden's gun being here?"

He took slow steps toward her, and with every step, she moved to the side, keeping what distance she could between them. "Are you kidding? In this neighborhood? Stolen guns show up around here every day. I'll drop it in a dumpster or give it to some homeless guy."

How many minutes had it been? Fifteen? Twenty? *Keep him talking.* He thought he was invincible. Smarter than her. *Play to that ego.*

She inched closer to the door. "What do I have that you feel you deserve, Ethan? How have I hurt you?"

"Cut the 'I'm your friend, let me help you' act." He tucked the gun into the back of his pants and picked up the drapery cord from the bed. He wrapped an end around each gloved hand and snapped it taut. He hadn't touched her yet, and she could already feel her throat constrict. *Get to the door.* "Dennis was right. You act like you're some kind of golden girl who can't do anything wrong. You know what's wrong? You getting the job I should have. You're going to be running the whole lab one day, and I'm just going to be that guy who keeps getting passed over, time and again."

Her shaking fingers curled around the doorknob behind her. "I asked you if you were okay with me being your boss. You wished me luck."

Once step closer. "*I'm* supposed to be running the show. I've worked there longer and harder than you, and Mac never seemed to notice. He kept putting 'needs to work on' memos in my file, even recommended me for a psych eval once. Said I didn't always react appropriately to stressors." *You think?* Her fingers found the lock above the knob. "Dennis was going to recommend me for promotion. And then pretty little Lexi comes along and charms her way in with the top brass." One step closer. Another step. She could hear the excited pattern of his breathing now. "I want you to understand that you're not that smart. You're not gifted. You're lucky. You don't deserve what you've got. You lost evidence at one crime scene. Incompetent! You rattle on about curtains opening and closing like you're crazy."

"You wanted to undermine my authority. You set me up to look bad and to doubt my abilities."

"And it was working. You weren't going to last until the New Year." He was close enough that she could feel the heat coming off his body. "And then you solved those murders. You got Dennis fired. You got him arrested. I was never going to be liked the way you are. I was never going to be golden." Was that the elevator she heard whining and creaking in the distance? That wretched, ancient noise was the sound of hope. "I just wanted you to know it was me before I killed you and put me out of my misery. After a few weeks of mourning, Mac will be looking for a new supervisor to run the lab. The team will be looking for leadership. With you gone, they'll look to me. You didn't save the lab. You couldn't even save yourself."

How many minutes had passed? Her grip tightened around the lock. Ethan could torment her. He could even try to kill her. But he wasn't going to win.

"You really are a dumb criminal, Ethan. Telling me everything. I know what you've done. I know you killed TNT to lure me here and plant the tainted evidence. I know your motive. I will make one hell of a witness when I testify against you."

He laughed. "Who's a dead woman going to tell?"

"You were a decent criminalist, but a lousy criminal. Any first-year CSI will figure out what you've done here."

The instant he heard the door unlock behind her, Ethan lunged. She kicked at the door, but instead of freedom, he threw her to the floor. Before she could scramble to her feet, he looped the cord around her neck and dragged her back into the middle of the room.

Lexi clawed at his hands, twisted her body like a fish caught on a line. But the cord only grew tighter. Her breath locked up in her chest. She gasped for air, but nothing happened. She couldn't scream. Tighter and tighter. Her eyes seemed to swell from the pressure. The beiges of the room faded into murky shadows. She was choking. Dying.

She never saw the door swing open. But she heard the bam of the knob striking the wall. She heard the crunch of fist on bone.

And suddenly she was free.

Lexi collapsed to her knees, clawing at the ligature around her neck. Suddenly, there were other hands there, unwinding the rope from where it had embedded into her skin. She dragged in a noisy gasp of air, whimpering at the pain in her neck, rejoicing as her lungs filled with oxygen again.

"Blue! *Pass!* Guard the bad guy."

As oxygen returned to her brain, she blinked the world back into focus. She was surrounded in warmth, sitting in Aiden's lap on the edge of the bed. His fingers gently inspected what she expected was a pretty nasty mark around her neck. She caught his hand, found his blue eyes and smiled. "I'm okay. I knew you'd come if I gave you enough time. You said you'd always be there for me."

Aiden nodded, pressed a hard kiss to her lips, then hugged her tightly against him. "I'm just glad I finally got to punch somebody."

She glanced down at Aiden's feet. Ethan lay on the floor, his hood down, his mask gone, his broken nose bleeding. Sucker punch. Blitz attack. Whatever it was called, Aiden hadn't needed his weapon to lay Ethan out flat and free her. Ethan's moaning elicited no sympathy from her. He'd done the same to her and worse. He'd killed an innocent woman, attacked Aiden, threatened Blue and had tried to kill her more than once. With his hands zip-tied behind his back, he wouldn't hurt anyone again.

Not that he was going anywhere. Blue lay on

the floor, only a few inches from his face. If
Ethan so much as twitched, Blue would take a
chunk out of him just as enthusiastically as he
went after his Kong.

ONCE THEY'D BEEN cleared by EMTs, the rest of
her team had shown up to process the right crime
scene, and Ethan had been put in the back of a
police car by their new friends Hud and Keir,
Lexi and Aiden had driven home and fallen into
bed together. They slept in each other's arms for
several hours. Then they got up to shower and
eat an early breakfast and went back to bed. This
time, they made love, celebrating their survival,
exploring the unshakable trust they shared, loving and protecting each other in the most beautiful way.

Afterward, sleep claimed them again. Lexi
wasn't sure if it was a matter of minutes or hours
that she'd slept on top of Aiden's chest, tucked
against him with their hearts beating together,
in the most secure place she'd ever known, when
she heard Blue barking an alarm. Someone was
at the house. The front door was opening.

Aiden must have already heard someone jim-
mying the door, or a key turning in the lock, because by the time she had slipped from beneath
the covers to grab her clothes, Aiden already had
his jeans on and his gun drawn and was racing
down the hallway.

"Oh, hell!" She heard Aiden curse. "Blue! *Sitz!*"

Sit. Not attack. Not a threat.

"Haven't you ever heard of knocking?" Aiden accused.

"I did. Nobody answered. I remembered the key hidden in the mailbox and decided to let myself in."

She knew that voice. Joy surged through her as Lexi tugged down her pajama shirt and ran through the house to greet her big brother. "Levi!"

Her brother opened his arms and she launched herself into his embrace. "Hey, kiddo."

"Welcome home! Oh, it's so good to see you. Merry Christmas. Welcome home!"

Her toes hit the floor as he set her down. "You said that already." He frowned at the mark on her neck. "Hey, what happened here?"

"It's work stuff. Aiden saved my life. We caught the bad guy. It's all good." She waved aside his concern and turned his face down to hers. She pushed off his khaki stocking cap and inspected him from his buzz cut of hair down to the snow still clinging to his Marines-issue boots. He looked good. Tired, but fit. His tan was darker, his eyes lined a little more deeply, but it felt wonderful to finally have him home. "You've already walked through the snow, haven't you?"

He nodded. "I love the cold air. Feel like I can breathe here." They were still gathered in the hallway. Levi in his digitized camo uniform, Lexi in her jammies, and Aiden in…

Oh, no. Her cheeks heated with embarrassment.

Levi grinned, seeing the exact moment when she realized that she and Aiden looked like they'd just made love. He flicked at the tag at the back of her neck. "Your shirt's on inside out, sis." Then he inclined his head toward Aiden. "And you, my friend, have no shirt on at all."

Aiden tucked the gun into the back of his jeans. "I can explain. It's been an interesting month. Things have changed."

Levi arched an eyebrow. "Seriously? You think I care that you've been in bed with my sister? Now, some other guy—"

"There is no other guy." Lexi stood beside Aiden, linking her arm with his, wondering if this was the moment that Aiden backed away from the closeness they shared. Because he owed something to her family, and he didn't believe that loyalty and nobility and love could all go hand in hand.

"I know that. Do you?" Levi stooped down to pet Blue, giving the dog a thorough wrestle and tummy rub. "Get a clue, you two. I've been throwing you together from three thousand miles away every way I could think of—telling you he needs a square meal at least once a week, telling you she needs someone to rotate her tires, shovel snow, look after her?" Levi pushed to his feet and winked at Aiden. "You've had the hots for her ever since she sprouted breasts—"

"Levi—!"

"And there's no man I'd trust to love her any better than I know you can."

He cupped Lexi's cheek in his big hand and smiled. "There's not a better man in the world, Lex. Have you two figured it out yet?"

"I have. I'm in love with Aiden." She tilted her gaze up to Aiden's. "I've been in love with you for a long time. The evidence is in my journals upstairs. I know you didn't want me to love you. That you just wanted us to be friends. But we're both. I'm closer to you than anyone else in the world, Aiden. You're my best friend and the man I love."

Levi crossed his arms over his chest and dared Aiden to better that speech. "You?"

"I kind of wanted to tell her how I felt first." He brushed a lock of hair off her cheek and tucked it behind her ear. "I love you, Lexi Callahan. I've never loved anybody else. I just didn't think I was the best man for you—"

"Shut up." Lexi rose up on her toes and wound her arms around Aiden's neck and kissed him. "I've never loved anyone else, either. You're the best man—the only man—for me."

Levi chuckled behind them. And when she turned to face him, her big brother was grinning from ear to ear. "My work here is done."

He pulled his cap back on and lifted his duffel bag onto his shoulder.

"Where are you going?" Lexi stopped him at the door. "You just got home. Tomorrow is Christmas."

"Hotel. Don't worry. I'll be back for the festivities tomorrow morning. But I think you two have some celebrating you need to do tonight."

"I love you, Levi."

He leaned down to kiss her cheek. "Love you, too, kiddo."

He dropped the bag to shake hands with Aiden and pull him in for a quick hug. "Love you, bro."

"Love you."

"Densest couple I ever met." Levi headed out the door to his rental car, grumbling as the door closed behind him. "The Marine's always got to come in and save the day."

Once he was gone, Aiden and Lexi faced each other. Aiden loved her. Nothing seemed impossible to her now. "I think the K-9 Patrol saved the day just fine, without any help from the Marines."

"I had a lot of help from the crime lab."

She tangled her fingers together with his and backed toward the couch, pulling him along with her. "I had such a crush on you growing up. After Mom and Dad died, I was lost in grief and anger and pain. I needed you to be my friend. And you were. Then I went off to college and life happened, and we never got the chance to be something more."

"After your folks were killed, I was just lost. Patrick and my stepmoms weren't family to me—you and Levi were. I couldn't lose that." He set his gun on the table beside the sofa and recaptured her hand, tugging her to him. "It took nearly losing you to admit how deep my feelings go, how I never want to lose you again."

"For a cop and a criminalist—"

"Senior criminalist," he corrected, kissing her smile.

"We weren't very bright." She glanced at the door as they heard Levi driving away. "I can't believe that thickheaded Marine was playing matchmaker all along."

"I see the light now. I'm not losing my foster family. I'm gaining a family of my own."

"You're not going to lose me, Aiden Murphy. I love you."

"I love you, Lex. I need you. You're the only Christmas present I ever truly wanted."

"So I can take back those gifts under the tree?"

"You know what I want under the tree?" He scooped her up in his arms, then sat with her on the couch. A few minutes later, they were on the rug, kissing beneath the tree.

"Tell me one thing." He paused and lifted his head, looking far too serious as he waited for her to speak. "Did you really notice when I sprouted breasts?"

He laughed, palmed said breast and proceeded to make love to her. "Oh, yeah. I most certainly did."

* * * * *

Don't miss the next book in USA TODAY
bestselling author Julie Miller's
Kansas City Crime Lab series,
on sale next year, only from Harlequin Intrigue!

Get 4 FREE REWARDS!

We'll send you 2 FREE Books plus 2 FREE Mystery Gifts.

Harlequin Presents books feature the glamorous lives of royals and billionaires in a world of exotic locations, where passion knows no bounds.

FREE
Value Over
$20

YES! Please send me 2 FREE Harlequin Presents novels and my 2 FREE gifts (gifts are worth about $10 retail). After receiving them, if I don't wish to receive any more books, I can return the shipping statement marked "cancel." If I don't cancel, I will receive 6 brand-new novels every month and be billed just $4.55 each for the regular-print edition or $5.80 each for the larger-print edition in the U.S., or $5.49 each for the regular-print edition or $5.99 each for the larger-print edition in Canada. That's a savings of at least 11% off the cover price! It's quite a bargain! Shipping and handling is just 50¢ per book in the U.S. and $1.25 per book in Canada.* I understand that accepting the 2 free books and gifts places me under no obligation to buy anything. I can always return a shipment and cancel at any time. The free books and gifts are mine to keep no matter what I decide.

Choose one: ☐ **Harlequin Presents Regular-Print** (106/306 HDN GNWY)   ☐ **Harlequin Presents Larger-Print** (176/376 HDN GNWY)

Name (please print)

Address   Apt. #

City   State/Province   Zip/Postal Code

Email: Please check this box ☐ if you would like to receive newsletters and promotional emails from Harlequin Enterprises ULC and its affiliates. You can unsubscribe anytime.

Mail to the **Harlequin Reader Service:**
IN U.S.A.: P.O. Box 1341, Buffalo, NY 14240-8531
IN CANADA: P.O. Box 603, Fort Erie, Ontario L2A 5X3

Want to try 2 free books from another series! Call 1-800-873-8635 or visit www.ReaderService.com.

*Terms and prices subject to change without notice. Prices do not include sales taxes, which will be charged (if applicable) based on your state or country of residence. Canadian residents will be charged applicable taxes. Offer not valid in Quebec. This offer is limited to one order per household. Books received may not be as shown. Not valid for current subscribers to Harlequin Presents books. All orders subject to approval. Credit or debit balances in a customer's account(s) may be offset by any other outstanding balance owed by or to the customer. Please allow 4 to 6 weeks for delivery. Offer available while quantities last.

Your Privacy—Your information is being collected by Harlequin Enterprises ULC, operating as Harlequin Reader Service. For a complete summary of the information we collect, how we use this information and to whom it is disclosed, please visit our privacy notice located at corporate.harlequin.com/privacy-notice. From time to time we may also exchange your personal information with reputable third parties. If you wish to opt out of this sharing of your personal information, please visit readerservice.com/consumerschoice or call 1-800-873-8635. **Notice to California Residents**—Under California law, you have specific rights to control and access your data. For more information on these rights and how to exercise them, visit corporate.harlequin.com/california-privacy.

HP21R2